RUNAWAY POET

Myra Nagel

ISBN 13:978-1480149915

This book is dedicated to
all abused, neglected, and abandoned children
to their foster families,
and to those professionals and volunteers
who work to make their lives better.

All author proceeds from the sale of this book,
both paperback and electronic,
will be donated to

Voices for Kids

of Southwest Florida,

an organization dedicated to
improving the lives
of abused, neglected, and abandoned children
who come under the protection
of Southwest Florida's courts.

OTHER BOOKS BY MYRA NAGEL

FICTION

DOWNSIDE SEVEN, 2012

NON-FICTION

DELIVER US FROM EVIL, 1999

JOURNEY TO THE CROSS, 1996

www.myranagel.com

Chapter One

The resumption of Pop Warner football created an illusion of normalcy at Carmalita Field on this September Saturday in 2004, the year of the infamous Hurricane Charley. But *normal* was a long way off.

It had been over a month since the forecasted Category Two storm wound up to a Cat Four, took an early turn in from the Gulf of Mexico, and tracked twenty miles up the large bay named Charlotte Harbor, catching The Weather Channel flat footed. Within a few wild hours, it destroyed 27,000 homes, racked up damages exceeding three billion dollars, and left our small city of Punta Gorda looking like a war zone. August 13, it was. Friday the Thirteenth. I'm not kidding. The town would recover, of course–at least the damaged buildings would. The inner storms were another matter

A mini-tempest whirled in my head as I climbed past a short line of football moms in the makeshift stands. This was the first time I'd come. I'd wanted to give Ben a little time before I showed up to watch his humiliation.

Out on the field the Midgets took their positions, their scrawny young bodies muscled up with padding. I spotted Ben quickly–not in the game, of course, but hunched on the end of the bench as far away from the other players as he could manage. How his dad could ever have thought this experience would be good for him was a mystery to me.

At fifteen, Ben was at the top of the age bracket for the Midget Division, so he was the oldest kid on the team—and by far the worst. Any halfway decent player his age would want to play on the high school team—wouldn't be caught dead in the Pop Warner Program, a national youth football organization where kids start playing at age five and the coaches are mostly dads. But Ben was slight enough to squeak under the weight limit. And his father was trying to make a man of him

His twelve-year-old brother Jessie, on the other hand, had barely made it over the weight threshold, but he bragged that he was one of the "best on the team." Yes, there he was. In fact, he had the ball. The bigmouth mom next to me hollered, "Go, go go!" He did, making a first down. Although he was small for his age, Jessie was a natural athlete. It was one of the few things he did well.

The Charlotte Warriors had piled up a twenty-point lead when, wonder of wonders, Ben jogged onto the field, looking awkward, miserable, and tall. For the next two plays, he hovered at the edge of the action. Then his little brother hurled a perfect pass in his direction. Squinting against the sun, I held my breath as I watched it soar toward Ben, his body still as a photograph.

"Catch it!" I hollered. I'm not a big football fan, and I hate parents who make a scene on the stands, but I couldn't help myself. "Get it!" The pass was so perfect, he couldn't miss. Unless he ducked, which is exactly what he did a split second before the ball should have sailed into his hands. The moms and dads in the stands let out a collective moan as the football flew past him and died on the grass.

"What's that kid doing out there?" shouted Bigmouth next to me. I wanted to punch her right under the *Charlotte Warriors MOM* on her T-shirt. Or maybe it was Jessie I wanted to punch–for mortifying his brother on purpose. Or their dad for putting Ben in this impossible situation. But really and truly, the person I was most furious with was . . . me. Anna Sebastian.

How had I ever let myself get into the middle of this soap opera? What self delusion allowed me to believe I could make a difference in the lives of kids like Ben and Jessie Tolliver, who had bounced from foster home to foster home, getting kicked out of most of them? Whatever made me think that other people's children could fill the aching hole Alistair had left in my life? *Irrational self-*

confidence, hopeless idealism, and certifiable insanity. Oh, and loneliness.

It was the newspaper story that had hooked me. The headline, *Kids in Crisis,* caught my eye on a day when I'd been feeling even more down than usual. The article highlighted the nation-wide program called CASA–Court Appointed Special Advocates. In Florida, these advocates were called Guardians Ad Litem, but they weren't guardians in any real sense. In plain English, the title meant "guardian during the litigation." Throughout the legal proceedings, these "guardians" acted as a voice for abused and neglected children in the court, where life-changing decisions were made for them in their absence.

I read the whole article twice. *I could do that*, I thought. I knew how to cope with problem kids. Or so I thought. And my first few cases had involved pre-schoolers. A piece of cake, relatively speaking. Then I'd asked for older youth. *Big mistake*, I thought as I turned to Bigmouth and answered her question about what that kid was doing out there. "He's trying to learn the game. He's never played before."

"Oh!" she said, flustered. "He's your son?"

I wanted to embarrass her by saying yes, but instead I told the truth–or at least part of it. "I'm a friend of the family."

"I didn't mean . . . ." Bigmouth clearly didn't know where to go with this sentence, so she started over. "He'll catch on, I'm sure."

"Maybe," I said, watching him sulk near the edge of the playing field. From the sidelines, one of the coaches shouted something at him. Ben shrugged, then raised his arms half-heartedly and moved closer to the action.

The mom on the other side of Bigmouth nudged her and asked, "Who's that coach? I haven't seen him before."

"I don't know," Bigmouth said. Her raised eyebrows said she'd thought she knew absolutely everybody involved with this team. "He must be new."

After ten more minutes of torture, the coach replaced several players, including Ben, who moved toward the bench with a lot more spring in his step than he'd shown when he walked out onto the field.

To cap off the misery of the morning, an official called a penalty on Jessie early in the second half. *Keep your cool, Jessie,* I murmured under my breath. I repeated the words like a mantra--as if it could help. It didn't. Beet red, he stomped over to the official, who pointed firmly toward the bench, and I had a terrible premonition of what would happen next. As I covered my eyes and peeked through my fingers, Jessie wound up like a prizefighter and slugged the man right in his oversized gut.

I stood up and headed for the porta-potty so I wouldn't have to listen to Bigmouth's commentary. I didn't even want to admit I knew the kid.

Chapter Two

When I returned to the game, Jessie sat hunched on the bench with his back to the field, his crewcut dark head buried in his knees. Though I couldn't see his face, I knew from past experience the fury and frustration it held. Fury and frustration were the story of his life.

Jessie didn't do many things well, but in sports he was truly gifted. Even so, he always seemed to manage to find some way to blow it. He didn't do it on purpose; he truly didn't. He had Fetal Alcohol Spectrum Disorder—FASD. His mother's boozing during her pregnancy damaged his brain. Added to that was the trauma of foster care, which Jessie entered at age six. By the time the Tolliver brothers landed in the experienced hands of George and Candy Owen a year ago—the same time I was assigned to their case—six previous sets of foster parents had turned them back to DCF with a pile of complaints about Jessie. The kid stole, lied, disrupted his special-education classes, refused to do his homework, kicked or bit his friends, and terrorized everyone around him with violent and unpredictable tantrums.

Fortunately, the Owens had seen this kind of behavior before. Less than two weeks after Ben and Jessie were placed with them, Candy carted Jessie off to the pediatrician and requested testing for Fetal Alcohol Syndrome. Bingo. The diagnosis didn't cure him, of course. There's no cure. But once they identified the problem, Candy and George began to create the kind of structure and order that helped Jessie cope with his handicap. Then last February, about the time he was showing real improvement, his biological parents appeared out of nowhere—back together after years of separation, free of drugs and alcohol, and determined to get their sons back. After five months of jumping through hoops for DCF, Tiffany and Gordon Tolliver gained permission to take their children home for a trial period. A month later, Hurricane Charley tore through their rented duplex, and they were forced to move into a tiny FEMA travel trailer parked in their front yard. Structure and order went out the window, and Jessie started losing ground. Now he had outdone himself by slugging a referee.

As I watched Jessie huddle on the sideline, my heart went out to him. He probably didn't understand why he'd been benched. Like many FASD kids, he didn't grasp the relationship between cause and effect. But try to explain that to a football coach.

For the rest of the game, Jessie sat backwards in his body clench. When the agony finally ended, he stormed past his celebrating teammates and blew by the bleachers without a glance at me. Ben trudged off the field a few minutes later, but I wasn't going to let him pretend I wasn't there. I hollered at him, and he dragged to a stop to let me catch up. Exercise and sunshine brought out a smattering of freckles on his fair skin and accented the small V-shaped scar on his cheek. His sweaty blonde hair nearly eclipsed his eyes.

"Don't say it, Anna," he muttered. "I know I stink, so don't bother lying to me." It was probably the closest I'd ever heard him come to expressing his true feelings.

"It just takes time, Ben," I told him. "You've only been playing a few weeks."

"Save your breath." He turned away and slumped toward the stands.

Undaunted, I called after him. "I'll buy you a Coke later if you like."

"Not today."

With a sinking heart, I watched him clamber up the far side of the metal stands and stretch himself flat on the top bleacher. Face turned away.

Behind me, a polite male voice asked, "Ma'am?" Turning, I looked into the face of the new coach. He wasn't as tall as he had seemed on the field—probably only three or four inches taller than my own 5'6"—but he was slender and moved like an athlete. "Are you Ben's mother?" he asked, pointing toward the prone figure on the bleacher.

"Oh, no," I said quickly. "I'm . . . ." I decided to level with him. "I'm his Guardian Ad Litem." As briefly as I could, I explained what that meant.

He frowned. "He's a foster kid then?"

"No, he lives with his parents, but the family is still under the supervision of the court."

"He doesn't much act like he wants to be here."

I tried for a laugh, but it came out a snort. "You got that right. His father is making him play."

Nodding toward the motionless figure on the bleachers, he asked, "Does he always hang around after the games?"

"He and his brother have to wait for his dad to pick up their carpool." Gordy Tolliver worked a half day on Saturday.

"His brother?"

"Jessie. The kid who slugged the referee."

"Ah." I waited for him to make a snide remark or to lecture me about Jessie's attitude, but instead he asked, "How long before their dad gets here?"

"Forty-five minutes, give or take."

Still watching Ben, he said, "If he's willing, I could work with him while he waits. Learning how to handle a ball can do wonders for a young man's ego."

I winched my jaw off the ground and studied him, wondering why he would single Ben out for special help. The coach wasn't exactly handsome. His nose was a bit too dominating, his mouth a little too wide. And his reddish blonde hair was even curlier and less manageable than mine. Still, the total combination was not unpleasant. "I don't think his family could pay you," I told him.

"Oh, no fee." He made a gesture like an official signaling a kick is no good. "It's only forty-five minutes," he added with a smile. "I'm Jack Braxton, by the way."

I found myself returning his smile. "Anna Sebastian. Are you serious about working with him?"

"Sure. I'll go talk to him. See if I can persuade him to get his body in motion." Transfixed, I watched Ben glance up at him, listen a few minutes, then shuffle after him, looking like he'd rather be somewhere else. Almost anywhere else.

I decided to stick around the park until the boys' father came so I could tell him about the new development in Ben's life. In the meantime, I watched the coaching session. When Ben missed a pass that was so gentle a six-year-old should have caught it, Coach Jack took the boy's hands in his own and placed them on the ball, talking the whole time. A grueling twenty minutes later and at least as many misses and fumbles, Ben finally caught one. He actually caught it! The coach threw his hands up in a gesture of triumph. Ben's posture straightened.

Later, as I waited in the parking lot for Gordy Tolliver, Ben and Coach Jack strolled up together. "If you can get to Tuesday's practice early," the coach was saying, "we could have some time to work out."

"I always get here early," Ben said with obvious disgust. "Weekdays, we ride with our neighbor on her way to work, so we come way early. No choice."

"Great! I'll see you then."

"Whatever." Ben turned his back and slouched toward the street.

"He has the makings of a decent player," the coach told me. "There's hope."

Hope. I tried to remember how long it had been since that word passed through my brain, but before I had time to count the years, Gordy drove up. Jessie, who'd been squatting on the gravel ignoring me, dove into the pickup the minute it stopped moving, and Ben climbed in behind him. I waved to get their father's attention.

Rolling down his window, Gordy gave Jack a puzzled smile when I made introductions and explained the coach's offer to work with Ben. But he reached out to shake Jack's hand. "Thanks," he said. "Sure appreciate it."

Watching the truck drive away, Coach Jack asked, "Will you be here Tuesday?"

"No, but I'll try to make the next game."

"See you Saturday then."

Unfortunately, by the time Saturday rolled around, a Pop Warner football game was the last thing on anyone's mind. Incredible as it seemed, yet another hurricane—this one named Jeanne—blew through the area that day. Compared to Charley, Jeanne was child's play, but it shut the whole city down for the weekend. So it was the following Thursday evening before I made it back to Carmalita Field.

Drills had already ended when I clambered up the bleachers, and the scrimmage was under way. "Your boy's out there," Bigmouth said, pointing as I slid in.

Sure enough, Ben stood awkwardly on his own forty-yard line, wide open. Clearly no one thought it necessary to guard him. The ball carrier glanced his way, then tried a pass to a player who was surrounded by half the opposing team. It was incomplete, of course. A yard lost. The next play went down the same way. Two more yards lost.

Third down. Ben raised his hand and moved in closer, the first time I'd ever seen him indicate a speck of interest in the game. Bigmouth's son dropped back, searched frantically for an open receiver, looked at Ben, hesitated, then tossed the ball his way.

The pass could not have been better aimed. I held my breath as I watched Ben extend his arms and cup his hands the way Coach Jack had drilled him. The ball made contact. To my amazement, Ben held onto it and tucked it down under his arm. Without thinking, I was on my feet screaming worse than Bigmouth. She yelled too–she really wasn't that bad, I decided. Ben got tackled, but who cared? He had caught it. A first down! A couple teammates slapped him on the back, and I felt a sudden tightness in my throat.

After it was all over—after the practice ended, after I embarrassed Ben by hugging him, and after Jessie stomped away from the bench with his face turned away—I waited near the parking lot to congratulate Ben one more time and to thank his coach. The two of them walked up together, and Ben sprinted to his dad's waiting truck. I wondered if he would tell his father he made a first down. As the pickup pulled away, Coach Jack turned to me, beaming like he'd caught the pass himself. "Told you we'd make a ball player out of him," he said.

"I don't know how to thank you," I said.

He seemed to consider this. "Well, you could start by joining me for a drink—and dinner if you haven't eaten. I think Harpoon Harry's is still closed, but a lot of the restaurants in north Port Charlotte have opened up again. How about Chili's? Or do you have someone waiting for you at home?"

"No I don't," I said. "And I ate before practice, but a drink sounds great."

In the pit of my stomach, a small yellow butterfly fluttered its wings.

Chapter Three

As Jack and I drove north over the bridge into Port Charlotte, Punta Gorda's neighbor across the Peace River, we relived Ben's great catch, then lapsed into silence. "You don't sound like a Florida native," he said after a bit.

"No. I moved here from Chicago five years ago." Small talk.

The trouble with small talk is that, for me, it never turned out very small. I envied people who could carry on cheerily about husband, kids, house, job. But how could I make bright conversation about my husband leaving me for another woman? Or about moving to Port Charlotte to live with my mother, who had Alzheimer's Disease even though she was still in her 50's? I tried to keep it light, but Jack responded with so much sympathy I ended up spilling my guts. And when he told me he had moved to Punta Gorda after his wife was killed in an auto accident, my own problems didn't seem as huge as I'd thought they were.

Jobs were a safer topic, but part-time bookkeeping at Charlotte Family Practice sure wasn't very exotic. It fit my needs though. I'd had to put Mom in a nursing home after she started parading around the neighborhood naked. And when her physician, Dr. Johansen, discovered I had bookkeeping experience, he offered me a job, promising that its twenty-five hours a week could be as flexible as I needed.

Jack, I learned, had studied Computer Science at the University of Georgia and eventually started a business named Computer Doc in Atlanta. "I sold it after my wife died," he told me. "I thought a change of scenery might help. Right now I'm just free-lancing. Might hire myself out to someone one of these days or maybe lease a shop and set up Computer Doc again. Sometime. Anyway, I'm keeping my head above water so far." His voice had taken on a flat quality, like he could barely muster the energy to talk about it.

I was hunting words for a sympathetic response when we pulled into Chili's parking lot. Being one of the few restaurants that had reopened after Hurricane Charley, it was busier than usual for a Thursday evening in late September. We made our way to a table as far from the piped music as we could manage. I ordered Bud Light; Jack ordered iced tea. A surprise.

"So what made you decide to volunteer as a Guardian Ad Litem?" he asked after the waitress left. "You didn't have enough heartache and pain in your life already?"

"Hardly that."

"You just like banging your head against a stone wall."

"Yeah, and when I get tired of doing that, I enjoy putting my thumb in a vice and squeezing till I scream."

He smiled. "Plus you wanted to save the world."

"Not the world."

"Two kids."

"I wish." I met his eyes. They were blue as the Gulf of Mexico. "In reality though, if I could make this much difference"—I held my thumb and index finger a quarter inch apart—"I'd think it was worth it."

"It's nice, anyway," he said. "To want to."

My cheeks warmed at the compliment, and I felt like a fraud. "It's not that I'm a big do-gooder. I just . . . ." I debated how much to tell him.

"Just what?"

I had promised myself not to trust him. Or any man. When Drew walked out after five years of marriage, I'd vowed to keep my life testosterone free for a good long while. Now, though, the curiosity on Jack's face threw me. How long had it been since a guy actually seemed interested in things that mattered to me? "You want the truth?" I asked finally.

"The truth."

I let it out in a long sigh. "I was missing my stepson, Alistair."

"Ah."

When he didn't say more, I added, "He was thirteen—between Jessie and Ben."

He studied me, head cocked. "And you thought you could, well, not exactly replace him, but maybe . . . ."

"I knew I couldn't replace him," I said quickly, and I heard the defensive note in my voice. "I just thought establishing a relationship with someone closer to Alistair's age might help take away the loneliness. And I'd learned a lot about how to deal with a rebellious and troubled kid. My stepson was one belligerent eight-year-old when Drew and I got married, but I finally broke through the wall he built around himself, and we got to be good buddies. So I requested a case that involved teens."

"Do you ever see him? Alistair?"

I shook my head. "Drew got married the minute our divorce was final, and he persuaded me it would be better for his son if I dropped out of his life. Alistair still sees his own mother, and now he has a new stepmother. How many mothers does one boy need?"

He was quiet a long time. "You still miss him." It wasn't a question.

I sought his eyes, but they had taken on a far-away look. "I guess I don't have to tell you about missing someone," I said.

"No." He still avoided my gaze.

"How long since your wife died?"

"Two years and four months."

I suspected he could supply weeks and days if I asked. "What was her name?"

"Heather."

"You don't have children?"

He shook his head. "Shall we order some nachos?"

His quick change of subject told me I'd asked enough painful questions. "Sure."

He caught the waitress's eye and ordered. "Tell me more about Ben," he said after she left. "Besides that his dad is making him play football, I don't know much about him. You said he was in foster care for awhile. How come?"

"I'm obligated to protect the family's confidentiality, Jack. But speaking generally, I can tell you the Dependency Court doesn't get involved unless there's evidence that children are neglected or abused or unsafe in some way."

"Ben's parents were into alcohol and drugs, then cleaned up their act?"

I did a double take. How could he know that?

He seemed to sense my surprise. "Ben told me his brother has Fetal Alcohol Syndrome, so it sounds like there's a long history of substance abuse."

"You should be honored. He doesn't usually tell anyone that. In fact, he rarely talks about anything personal."

Jack shrugged. "It wasn't a long conversation; it just sort of happened. A younger boy gave Ben the finger as we were walking out toward the street together, and Ben mumbled, 'That's my dumb-ass brother.' Then I guess he felt like he should offer some kind of explanation, so he added, 'He got brain damaged because my mom drank too much when she was pregnant.'"

"Ben gets really frustrated with Jessie." I let out a deep sigh. "We all do."

Jack fiddled with the salt shaker on the table. "So have his parents really cleaned up their act?"

I answered carefully. "Speaking generally again, if the court had evidence that parents were using drugs, they wouldn't place children with them."

He mulled that over, then asked, "You agreed with the court's decision?"

"We're speaking generally, remember?"

"Yeah, but . . ."

"No buts." In truth, I'd had a knock-down, drag-out battle over the case with the DCF lawyer at the Judicial Review. It's not that I didn't think the boys' natural parents deserved a chance. Gordy had spent the last twelve months of an eighteen-month jail sentence in a substance abuse treatment center, and he genuinely seemed to have stayed clean since he got out. Besides, I liked the guy.

In contrast to a lot of the fathers who showed up in the Dependency Court, Gordy Tolliver was neat and clean-cut, his medium brown hair always neatly combed. The first time we met, he introduced himself with a friendly smile that showed a lot of lower teeth, and he met my gaze with steady dark eyes that somehow inspired my trust. He was polite in a way that didn't seem like an act, and he always expressed appreciation for "everything you are doing for us." True, he had a history of substance abuse, but the random drug screens required by DCF always came out negative, and he never acted high. I'd watched enough cases parade through the courtroom to recognize "impaired behavior," to use the Department's euphemistic label.

I didn't feel as confident about Tiffany, but her required random drug screens kept coming out negative, and I applauded anyone who managed to kick the habit. I just didn't think five months was a long enough trial period to justify removing Ben and Jessie from a foster home where they were both doing way better than they'd ever done before. I'd lost that battle though, and what's done was done.

I wished I could explain all this to Jack, but instead I said, "There's a terrible shortage of foster homes here." In fact, Candy and George Owen had accepted two more foster boys within days after Ben and Jessie moved out.

Jack traced aimless circles on the table with the salt shaker. "Ben seems OK–mentally, I mean. He doesn't have Fetal Alcohol Syndrome?"

"No, thank God." I brightened. "Actually he's very intelligent. Sometime you should ask him about his poetry."

"He writes poetry?"

The expression on his face made me laugh. "I have to admit I hardly understand a word of the poem he gave me, but it has a certain"—I searched for the word—"atmosphere. I have a gut feeling it's pretty good."

"Any chance I could read it?" Jack must have read the surprise on my face because he quickly added, "Just curious. It might help me relate to him better."

"I guess I could ask him if that would be OK"

"Thanks." His smile was so broad, I felt myself returning it. And wondering if Coach Jack Braxton could possibly be as good a guy as he seemed to be.

Chapter Four

On Saturday morning, I spent several hours with my mother. She had been refusing to eat, and I wanted to be present when Dr. Johansen came to see her. "Yummm, scrambled eggs," I told her, trying to coax some food into her mouth while we waited for the doctor. "Your favorite, Mother." Noting the alarmed confusion on her face, I quickly corrected myself and called her by her given name, Millie. The word *mother* had escaped my lips from long habit, but she no longer recognized me as her daughter. "Cereal looks good too, Millie. How about a bite?"

As I held the Cream of Wheat to my mother's mouth, Reba, her favorite nurse, hustled in. "Good girl, Millie," she said, patting Mom's knee. "I see Anna's taking care of you."

"My friend Anna," Mom said with a look of gentle sweetness that tugged at my heart.

"Whew! I sure appreciate you doing that," Reba said. "It's been wild around here."

"Worse than usual?" I asked, making conversation while I made another try at eggs.

"Ain't no such thing as 'usual' no more." she said with an unamused laugh. "Since the hurricane we've been filling every bed and then some with evacuees from nursing homes in Punta Gorda and the lower part of Port Charlotte. Top of that, rumors been flying around about missing prescription drugs in the area. None here at Hibiscus Villa I know of, but the Powers That Be are piling on new policies right and left. Making my life a zoo." Looking over her shoulder, she added, "Oh, here's the doctor."

Fortunately, Mom's eating problem turned out to be minor—a fungal infection in her mouth treatable with antibiotics—but I didn't get away in time to watch Ben play football. Later that afternoon, I was surprised and pleased when Jack called. He said he'd missed me at the game, and could we have dinner that night? It took me all of one second to say yes.

The evening turned out to be one of the nicest I'd had in a long time. After a delicious steak dinner, our conversation turned toward Ben. Jack asked if I'd brought the poem he had written, and I confessed I hadn't talked to him about it. Truth was, I hadn't quite believed Jack was serious about wanting to read it.

After I got home, I pulled Ben's poem out of the file where I kept everything relating to the Tolliver case. As I started rereading it, I found myself remembering what my relationship with Ben had been like in the days before I discovered his interest in poetry.

Back then, the two brothers had still been in foster care with the Owens. Jessie's FASD had been diagnosed, and I was beginning to understand him better, but my progress with Ben had been zilch. "How's it going?" I'd ask. Or "What have you been doing today?" He'd stare straight past me, twisting the one white ear of the otherwise black stuffed dog he often carried around.

I tried another tack. "What kind of vegetables do you hate the most? I can't stand broccoli; how about you?" A mute shrug. The silence had been deadly those first few meetings.

Undaunted, I made appointments to see both boys' school counselors. The news about Jessie was worse than I'd expected, and I began to get a clearer picture of the devastating effects of fetal alcohol. Ben's counselor delivered a different kind of surprise. Ben was making C's and B's in every subject but English. Virtually all his teachers described him as polite but withdrawn, never taking part in class discussion and uneven about completing homework. All of them remarked that he was smart and capable of doing better.

"What about his English grade?" I asked his counselor.

"He made an A," she said with a smile.

It hadn't taken me long to hunt down his English teacher, who described him as an insightful reader, good at remembering details, and gifted with words. She had awarded him A+ on his poetry unit and thought he showed exceptional talent. But she worried about his emotional state. He was a loner, and he rejected the attempts of other students to reach out to him. And his poetry, though brilliant, was eerily dark. She also observed that he never met her eyes. Even when she complimented him, which she did often, he would flush and say "thank you," but would not look at her.

After talking with this wonderful teacher, I'd had a brainstorm. Now as I thought back on that November afternoon nearly a year ago, I remembered my visit with Ben as if it had happened yesterday. I had perched on a padded wicker chair in the Owens' sunporch; Ben sprawled on the faded rattan couch with his ever-present stuffed dog in his lap. He stared out the floor-to-ceiling window, radiating boredom. Sunlight shone a halo on his too-long blonde hair, which for a change looked clean and fluffy. In the adjoining kitchen, Candy Owen worked at the sink, but she had closed the French doors to give us privacy.

I took a deep breath and ventured into uncharted territory. "I brought a poem for you today," I told Ben. "It's by Shel Silverstein. *The Missing Piece.*" His pupils slid sideways toward the slim book I held in my lap, but he didn't turn his head. I began reading aloud. "And as it rolled along, it sang this song. 'Oh, I'm lookin' for my missing piece, I'm looking for my missin' piece. Hi-dee-ho, here I go, Looking for my missin' piece.'"

Halfway through the poem, I noted in my peripheral vision that Ben had stopped gazing out the window and turned toward me. When I finished reading, he sat quietly for awhile, eyes fixed on something over my head. Then to my surprise, he said, "It seems like he's saying if you're not all together . . . I mean, if you don't have it all together—" His voice trailed off, and he turned back to the window, running his fingers absently over the stuffed dog's single button eye.

"If you don't have it all together, what?" I asked softly.

In a voice so low I had to strain to hear him, he said, "I guess he's saying that's not all bad."

After that, Ben began to open up a little. Oh, he wouldn't talk about anything personal, not even simple things like how his day had gone. And of course he wouldn't look me in the eyes. But we could read poems together and discuss them.

After Ben and Jessie went to live with their parents last July, holding a real conversation with him became more difficult. And after the hurricane hit a month later, it became darn near impossible. Like thousands of others whose homes had been ravished in the space of a few harrowing hours, the Tollivers suddenly found themselves homeless. Still, they were more fortunate than most. Responding to a plea from Melody Kahn, their DCF case manager, FEMA parked a small trailer in the front yard of their rented duplex within a few days after Charley roared through. It wasn't one of the sizeable mobile homes that eventually formed several huge "FEMA cities" in the Port Charlotte/Punta Gorda area, but rather a small travel trailer designed for weekending and short vacations. FEMA invested ten million dollars in these travel trailers as part of their earliest response to the disaster. Many people lived in these trailers for two years.

The first time I visited the family in their cramped new "home," Ben and I sat opposite each other in their small built-in dinette. A few feet away in the postage stamp space that passed for their living room, Jessie kept the TV at high volume. He wasn't watching it, but when I asked him to turn it off, he screeched. His mother puttered in the tiny kitchen, a couple feet from the dinette, ears hanging low.

Just as I was about to give up and go home, Ben ducked into his bedroom and came back with a piece of lined notebook paper, which he slid across the table without looking at me. With a smirk that never became a smile, he told me he had hidden it under the mattress of the bed he shared with Jessie so his nosey brother wouldn't find it. As usual, he'd brought the well-worn stuffed dog with him, and he fiddled with its floppy ears as I read.

THE DARK
by Ben Tolliver

Night comes like a tiger,
relentless and silent,
stalking its prey.

Whispers in darkness,
secrets behind closed doors
never heard in the light.

Dreams in dark bedrooms—
white bread and tuna.
Reach out with hope.

Wake to the nightmare.
The serpent shows its fangs
and slithers over the stones.

Wrath stomps on mercy.
The dogs howl,
break down the gates.

The lamb is abandoned,
the angel forsaken.
The Dark overcomes

When I finished reading, I looked up in amazement. "What does this mean—" I asked, "'—the serpent shows its fangs and slithers over the stones?'" Studying his fingers as they pulled the dog's white ear, Ben murmured that it was just words that popped into his head. I didn't press him. Discovering he liked poetry had been too big a breakthrough to risk blowing it. "Does that pup have a name?" I asked, trying for neutral territory.

"Floyd."

"He looks well loved," I commented, noting the way the plush head tilted a bit to the left.

"Mama gave him to me when I was four," he said without looking up.

Before I could respond, Jessie stormed into our midst ordering me to come outdoors to see what he was building, and my visit with his brother ended. Before I left the trailer, I told Ben I thought he had a lot of poetic talent. The part of his forehead I could see flushed, which I took as a sign that he was embarrassed but pleased.

Now as I reread Ben's poem, *The Dark,* I found it just as puzzling as I had the day he'd given it to me. Of one thing I was certain, however. These weren't just words that popped into his head. I hoped he would let me to show it to Jack, and I was glad I'd made arrangements to meet with him at Port Charlotte High on Wednesday. Ever since that frustrating experience of trying to hold a coherent conversation in the tiny trailer, I'd been visiting with both boys at their schools during recess or study hall. The administrative staff, grateful for anyone who took an interest in their problem students, was always happy to find us a private place to talk.

On Wednesday afternoon, that place turned out to be an empty conference room. Ben sauntered in and plunked himself down across the table from me. I'd learned from Alistair that conversation flowed a lot easier when we did something together, so I usually brought a game. Today, it was checkers. We played in silence for a good ten minutes before I asked, "How was your day?"

"Routinely bad," he said. A tiny upward curve of his lips told me he appreciated his small joke.

"What was the worst?"

"History. Miss Evangeline is mean."

"And the best?"

"Least bad," he corrected, studying the game board. "English, I guess." No surprise.

"Coach Jack told me you got to play for awhile in Saturday's game. He was proud of you."

"Doesn't take a lot to please him," he said, but his cheeks flushed as he made his next move.

"You like him, don't you?"

"He's pretty cool." He made another move before adding, "He gave us a ride home Saturday when Dad didn't show up."

"Us?"

"Me and Jessie and Harry Nagorski."

"What happened to your dad?"

Ben jumped three of my red pieces and collected them. "Had to stay late at work, I guess."

"How are things at home?"

"OK." Always the same non-answer when it came to personal subjects. I hadn't even been able to get a straight yes or no out of him last June when I'd asked him point blank if he wanted to stay with the Owens or move in with his natural parents. All he would say was, "My brother is determined to live with his real Mom and Dad, so I better go with him." Knowing he'd clam up if I pushed him, I'd learned to back off from questions he obviously didn't want to answer.

Distracted by these thoughts, I suddenly realized he had wiped out two more of my checkers. I shrieked, and he grinned. Then he said casually, "I wrote another poem." Digging a folded square of paper from his pocket, he handed it to me. My heart skipped a beat as I took in the words. I wished he would look at me.

"May I show this to Coach Jack?" I asked.

Taking advantage of my preoccupation, he jumped another of my men and added it to his pile. Then he murmured, "I doubt he'd be interested."

I took the jump he forced me to make. I was getting slaughtered, as usual. "I think he'd be very interested."

"I don't mind," he said, wiping out three more of my pieces, "if you want."

"I do want. And what about the other poem you gave me—*The Dark*? OK if I show him that one too?"

He frowned a moment, then shrugged. "Whatever." He captured my last piece and hooted in triumph.

Chapter Five

As I pulled my trusty white Ford Focus into the parking lot at Carmelita Field late Thursday afternoon, I couldn't wait to show Jack Ben's latest poem. My stomach was signaling it was time to eat, but Jack had invited me to dinner after the practice, so I downed a quick Snickers to tide me over. I didn't see Jack's blue Hyundai Santa Fe, so I read Ben's new poem over again while I waited.

FIRST DOWN
by Ben Tolliver

Pigskin missile, fast and deadly,
Faces on the bench all smirks and jeers
Duck!
"Where's your brain, Tolliver? Supposed to catch it!"
Hate this game. Hate dad for making me.
Jessie would have caught it. Naturally.

Back on the bench–chants and jeers,
"Baby Tolliver, 'fraid of the ball!"
I don't care.
Hate this game, hate dad for making me.
Hate the questions–"You even touch the ball?"
Who cares, who cares, who cares?

"Don't panic. Make your hands a cone.
Thumb and index fingers touch. Looking good."
Dropped it.
"Good try, good form. Just relax.
Don't give up. Takes practice. You can do it."

Good liar, that coach.

"Catch it at the numbers. Concentrate."
Contact! "Bring it to your chest!"
Pass complete! "First down!"
Anna red with cheering.
"Good catch," says Coach. "Nice job."
Good catch, nice job. Wish Mama was here.

Had I really been "red with cheering"? I pulled down my visor mirror and checked my reflection. My complexion wasn't excessively blushable. I had my mother's olive skin and brown eyes, and I could remember when her hair had been the color of dark chocolate like mine. I swiped at the curl that persisted in hanging down my forehead, then gave it up as hopeless. Surveying the lot again, I still didn't see Jack's Santa Fe, but it was after six, so I ambled toward the stands.

Bigmouth greeted me like an old friend. "Do you come to every practice?" I asked her.

"As many as I can," she answered with a laugh. She wore a blue Warriors T-shirt today.

I scanned the field, but couldn't pick out Ben or Jessie. Odd. I didn't see Coach Jack either.

"Where's your players?" she asked. "I don't see them out there."

"I don't either. Are they on the bench?"

"Not during drills."

"No, of course not. Maybe something happened with their carpool." But that couldn't be. I spotted Harry Nagorski on the sidelines with some of his pals, and Ben and Jessie always rode with his mom on weekdays. What could have happened to them? And where was Jack? "Have you seen the new coach?" I asked Bigmouth.

"Nope. And they're really short-handed today. It's been so tough this year. Hurricane Charley wiped out two of the men that were signed up to coach. Good thing the new guy showed up. A real gift from heaven."

"Yeah." Only where was he? I was beginning to worry.

By the time the drills ended, my worry had evolved into fury. Jack hadn't impressed me as irresponsible, but letting all these kids down was inexcusable. And what about our dinner date? And where were Ben and Jessie! It was just one stupid thing after another with them. I picked up my cell phone to call their home, but before I could punch the numbers, it chimed in my hand. It was Jack.

"Where are you?" I asked.

"At the airport. I'm not going to make the practice today, and I'll have to break our dinner date. A couple hours ago I got word that my aunt died, and I have to fly to Nebraska. I don't know exactly when I'll get back. I may have to stay awhile to straighten out some things. I'll call you when I know more."

"Oh, Jack, I'm so sorry." I was, but I was also relieved. At least he hadn't just blown off the kids' practice–or our date. He'd been caught up in circumstances beyond his control.

"Yeah, I'm sorry too. Will you tell Mike Peterson? You know who he is, don't you–the head coach? Biggest guy on the field."

"Of course."

"And Ben too."

"I'll tell him when I see him, but he never showed today. Jessie either."

"Really?" He was quiet a minute. "Something must have come up."

"I suppose." With those boys, there was always something. "Well, I'm really sorry about your aunt. And I hope you don't end up having too much stuff to straighten out."

"Me too. Thanks for understanding. I'll call you soon as I get back."

The disappointment sank in after I hung up, forcing me to admit how much I'd looked forward to seeing him--in spite of my resolution to keep my life testosterone-free for awhile.

My cell phone was still in my hand, so I poked the Tollivers' number. Four rings, then voice mail. Both parents would be working, of course—Tiffany at McDonald's and Gordy at Sunset Days Care Center, a nursing home just down the street from my mom's place. I'd hoped one of the kids would answer, but they didn't, so I left a message. "Hi Tiffany and Gordy," I said at the tone. "This is Anna Sebastian. I'm wondering why Ben and Jessie didn't come to football practice today. Call me, please."

Thoroughly depressed, I drove home.

A little before nine, Tiffany finally called. Her voice shook. "What have you done with my sons?"

I stared into the telephone receiver as if I hadn't heard it right. "What?"

"Ben and Jessie aren't here. I know DCF took them"

I didn't even attempt to answer her preposterous charge. "I'll be right over," I said.

Chapter Six

Sitting incongruously in the front yard of what remained of the Tollivers' duplex, the travel trailer was stifling and smelled of sweat. So much for the air conditioning repairman FEMA had promised to send. Tiffany faced me with her hands on her hips. One foot tapped a drumbeat on the vinyl floor, drawing my attention to her high-heeled flip-flops and her too short skirt. She still dressed like the blonde knockout she had undoubtedly been in her twenties, but years of alcohol and drug abuse had taken their toll. Her thinness bordered on anorexic, and makeup couldn't hide the bags under her smoldering blue eyes. "Where are my sons?"

Bewildered, I turned to her husband, who leaned against the kitchen counter, filling the narrow space between the sink and the built-in dinette. Gordy Tolliver was at least six feet tall, and he had kept the muscular physique he must have had as a young man.

"Thanks for coming, Anna," he said. "I'm sure we'll find the boys soon. I didn't really think we needed to bother you, but Tiffany insisted." Tossing a look at his wife that reminded me of an indulgent father, he made a "cool-it" gesture toward her, saying, "Easy, Tiff. Anna didn't take our kids."

"Bet she knows who did," she shot back.

I was too alarmed about the boys to respond to her accusation. "Ben and Jessie are missing?"

"As you well know." Folding her arms across her scantily clad chest, she glared at me. "Where did DCF take them?"

I bit back a caustic retort and struggled for a matter of fact tone. "The Department of Children and Families Services wouldn't do that."

"They did last time," she snapped.

"Last time" was five years ago when Ben was caught stealing food from Publix during a brief period when the children had been allowed to return to their mother after their first placement in foster care. Tiffany and Gordy had separated by this time. When the Protective Investigator found bare cupboards—and Tiffany stoned—he did indeed take the children, and they ended up back in the custody of the court.

"Last time was completely different," I told Tiffany. "If your case manager had any serious concerns about the safety of your children, she would have informed you."

Tiffany uncrossed her arms and picked at her fingernails. "Melody gave me a big lecture last week about how I got to make Jessie go to school. Like it's my fault he hates it." Averting her eyes, she added, "And he played hooky again yesterday." Her tone had lost some of its bravado.

I'd dealt with their DCF case manager enough times to realize that tact wasn't her long suit. With her angular frame, perennially windblown hair, and a tendency to sigh a lot, Melody Kahn projected the no-nonsense attitude of someone who was always in a hurry. Still, I knew her to be competent even if overworked.

"Unless the children were in immediate danger, it would take a court hearing to move them," I assured Tiffany. "DCF wouldn't just slip in and steal them away–certainly not for missing a few days of school." *And not with the chronic shortage of adequate foster homes we're facing.* I watched the anger drain from Tiffany's face, leaving it colorless. "How do you know Jessie played hooky?" I asked

.

She sank onto the convertible sofa beside a mountain of dirty clothes. "The school left a voice mail on my answering machine saying Jessie was absent. I guess they left one for Gordy at work too–they always do. When I got home and heard the message, I went out to hunt him down. I was gonna fry his ass, you know? I went over to that dumb dock he and Harry built on the other side of the lake. I was sure that's where he'd be, but he wasn't."

The "lake" was actually a small, shallow runoff basin, the kind that pop up all over coastal Florida. Polluted no doubt, but a place of wonder for young boys. Half a block down from the Tollivers' duplex, it lay tucked behind a small cluster of single-family homes where Jessie's friend Harry Nagorski lived. On the Nagorskis' side of the pond, lawns stretched to the water's edge, but the opposite shore was untended and overgrown, being too close to Dalton Street, the next block over, to leave room for houses. After the hurricane, Jessie and Harry had built a credible dock over there, using concrete blocks and blown-out roof boards they scrounged from the yards of absent neighbors.

Gordy moved a dirty dish from the counter into the sink. "I stopped on my way home from work to pick up the car pool like I always do on Thursdays, but Harry was the only one there. He told me Ben and his brother got into a big argument this morning because Jessie wouldn't get on the school bus with him. When I got home, there was no sign of either one of them. But we'll find them before long, I'm sure."

"You don't seem very worried," I said.

"Nah, they took stuff with them. Clothes." He shrugged. "They're kids, you know. I ran away from home a few times myself when I was their age. They'll be back when they get hungry enough."

There being no other place to sit in the eight-by-eight living room, I edged in beside Tiffany, consolidating enough of a pile of clothes to make space. "But you haven't seen either of them since morning?" I asked her.

She shook her head. "Ben called me at work with a headache. I suppose the big fight with Jessie gave it to him. He's like that–has headaches when he gets worked up. Anyway, I took him home. He didn't say a thing about Jessie cutting school. Probably figured his dad would blame him for letting his brother skip out."

"What time was that?"

"About one, I guess. My boss pitched a fit about me leaving right in the middle of Mickey D's lunch mob, so I just dropped Ben off at our corner."

"Have you checked with the neighbors?" I asked.

Tiffany stood up, twisted her hands uncertainly for a few moments, then walked over to the kitchen counter and stared out the window as if she could actually see something in the darkness. Gordy put a hand on her arm. "Ain't hardly anybody living around here now," Tiffany said. "Most everybody got wiped out in Charley. All those rich folks down by the pond went back up north to wait till somebody else cleans up their mess, you know? Except the Nagorskis. And these three duplexes on Erwin are all renters like us so they just moved out, God knows where. Only one who didn't is Vera Mosely across the street, but she didn't see nothing. I asked her already."

"What about the kids' friends?"

"I called the ones I know," Tiffany said. "Harry checked around too, but no one's seen them."

"At least that's what Harry told us," Gordy interjected. "But friends cover for each other, you know."

"What about Rachel?" I asked. A year younger than Ben, Rachel York had been Ben's foster sister while he was living with the Owens. She'd bounced in and out of enough foster homes to understand Ben's sullen moods, and she had befriended him from the beginning. Over time, she made cracks in the wall he had built around himself, and their friendship blossomed into romance.

"I called Mrs. Owen," Tiffany said. "She hadn't heard from Ben, and Rachel hadn't either."

An icy finger inched up my spine. "Have you called the police?"

Tiffany shook her head. "I thought you'd know where they are."

"You need to call them," I said. "And contact your case manager. If you can't reach Melody, leave her a voice mail." Like a subdued child, Tiffany reached for the phone on the kitchen counter behind her.

"Hold on," Gordy said, covering her hand with his. "There's no need to get the police involved." He came and sat beside me on the couch. "Look, Anna." I heard the pleading in his voice. "I'm sure those boys are just hiding out at somebody's house waiting for us to get over our mad. They might even be holed up in one of the empty places here in the neighborhood. They'll show up when their friends' parents figure out they're there—or when they get hungry enough."

"What do you mean, 'they're waiting for you to get over your mad'?" I asked.

He shrugged. "I warned Jessie I'd ground him for a month if he cut school again, and I told Ben I expected him to make sure his brother got on that school bus. Just give them a little time, OK? They'll come home, dragging their tails."

Steadying herself against the counter, Tiffany rocked back and forth, taking an occasional futile glance out the dark window. "What if something's happened to them?" she murmured.

"Nothing's happened," Gordy told his wife. His voice was calm, reassuring. "Ben's dresser drawers are half empty, and his girlfriend's picture is gone. I'm sure Jessie took clothes too–it's just that his stuff is such mess it's hard to tell."

Turning to me, he touched my arm. "Give us a break, Anna." His face looked strained. "That damn DCF is hounding us to death. They expect us to work so we can support our kids, but we also got to take substance abuse classes and parenting classes and anger management classes and see a counselor and show up for random drug screens at all hours of the day. Every time we turn around, we got to go in and fill out some form or show up in court for some damn thing or other. We're doing our best. Honest. We've kicked drugs–the tests prove it. We're trying to jump through all the hoops and still keep our jobs, OK? DCF will be all over us if they find out the boys ran away."

Everything he said was true. Florida law decreed that Dependency Court cases must reach "permanency"—reunion with parents, placement with a relative, adoption, etc.—within one year of the time the court became involved. The recent privatization of many DCF services had increased the case managers' load—and upped their incentive to turn over their cases as fast as they could. The result was exactly the situation Gordy described.

"Give us twenty-four hours," Gordy pleaded. "If them kids aren't back home by tomorrow afternoon, I'll call the police myself. Please, Anna, just twenty-four hours. OK?"

I felt for them both. They weren't perfect parents, but they were trying, and they seemed to be staying clean. They both had steady employment. Dishing burgers and scrubbing nursing home floors were minimum wage jobs, so they had to put in a lot of hours to make ends meet. They deserved a little slack, didn't they?

Gordy was right. If they called the police, Child Protective Services would almost certainly reopen their investigation of the family even if the boys were back home by morning. Jessie and Ben might even end up back in foster care, and they couldn't go back to the Owens' house; it was full. I wasn't sure either Jessie or Ben could cope with yet another foster home. Wasn't it reasonable to wait twenty-four hours?

I rubbed my hands over my face to break eye contact with Gordy. I needed to think. I turned all Gordy's arguments over in my head one more time, then made the only decision I could live with. "Everything you say makes sense," I said, "and it breaks my heart to say this, but I can't sit on the knowledge that two children are missing. I'll make the call if you don't want to, but my best advice is to call the police yourself."

Gordy whirled away from me and dropped his head into his hands. After a silence that seemed interminable, he got up, strode to the phone, dialed 911, and barked the pertinent information. "Cops will be here in a few minutes," he told his wife as he hung up. I wished them luck and left, feeling guilty for adding another layer of hardship to their lives.

The next morning, a nightmare about lost boys woke me at five thirty. It had begun with a dream about Ben and Jessie, but then the two boys merged into one, who morphed into Alistair. A figure who resembled my own dead father said, "It's all your fault."

At six, the rumble of the newspaper truck chased away any last hope of sleep. I turned on the coffee pot and staggered out to the driveway in my bathrobe to retrieve the Charlotte *Sun*. Its headline screamed at me.

BOY'S BODY FOUND IN POND
BROTHER MISSING

Chapter Seven

As I drove toward the Tollivers' trailer during my lunch break Friday noon, I found myself trying to busy my mind with something—anything—that would divert my attention from the monstrous horror that threatened to consume me. My eyes took in a woodpile that had been a home before Hurricane Charley hit, a scrap heap that had been a trailer, a house split in two by a fallen palm. The people who got hurt the worst in a natural disaster always seemed to be those who could least afford it. On the streets of Punta Gorda, rain-soaked mattresses and discarded furniture lay piled up like ruined lives along the curbs. A rag doll caught my attention, sprawled unnaturally on a mountain of soggy, pink insulation, and reality invaded my brain. Jessie was like that rag doll, cast onto the rubble of other people's mistakes. Now he was dead.

Forcing myself to focus on the road ahead, I turned into the ghost town where the Tollivers lived. Passing Dalton Street, a block before the Tollivers' corner, I glanced right. A Rescue Squad and several police cars lined the street near the tall grass and bushes that grew wild along the edge of the small pond where Jessie and his friend Harry had always loved to play. Yellow tape surrounded the area near their makeshift dock.

As I slowed to get a better look, the memory of my last visit with Jessie flashed through my mind. Last Monday, it had been. He'd given up his recess to meet with me at his school, skipping into the empty conference room with a chipped-tooth grin and a ready hug. No matter that on my previous visit he'd cussed me out in language that blistered my none-to-sensitive ears. His anger had passed as quickly as it came. His smile bought my forgiveness and I hugged him back, thinking of Alistair.

Now Jessie was gone from my life forever. Like Alistair.

And where was Ben? Would they find his body in the pond? The water wasn't deep and he knew how to swim, but those things hadn't saved Jessie. Still, Ben had taken clothes with him. That meant he was alive, didn't it?

An irritated honk behind me interrupted my rumination and hustled me on to my destination. A police car sat crosswise in the Tollivers' driveway, so I parked at the curb. Taking a deep breath, I forced myself to get out of my comfortable Ford Focus and walk into the pain.

On the threadbare convertible couch, Tiffany lay curled in near fetal position, her head resting on a gray-brown throw pillow, her body convulsed in sobs. At the built-in dinette, a plump, grim-faced woman was gradually transforming the mountain of clothing that had littered the sofa last night into neat piles. She nodded hello, and I recognized her as Harry Nagorski's mother.

"I'm so glad you're here," she said, standing up and greeting me like a drowning person who just spotted a lifeboat. "I'll leave you two to talk."

"I brought sandwiches and salad from Publix," I said.

Tiffany's sobbing had subsided a bit, and she looked at me listlessly. "Oh. Maybe later. Gordy might eat when he comes home."

"Where is he?"

Pausing on her way to the door, Mrs. Nagorski answered my question "He's over yonder where the police are working," she said, gesturing with her head toward the window above the sink. "Tiffany tried to get him to come home and so did the police, but he won't leave." She hurried out, closing the heavy door softly behind her.

Tiffany wrenched herself to a sitting position as I called her name, then buried her face in her knees. Not knowing what else to do, I slid onto the couch beside her and patted her shaking shoulders. "I'm so sorry," I murmured helplessly. "So, so sorry."

"My Jessie's dead," she choked, reaching for the box of Kleenex beside her. "I just can't believe it."

"Neither can I."

With the tissue still pressed to her nose, she whispered, "He was murdered, Anna!"

The word hissed like meat hitting a hot fry pan. "Murdered?"

"They found his body a couple hours after you left last night. Before they . . . took him away, they told us it looked like an accident, like he fell off the dock and hit his head on something. But this morning they came back and said somebody hit him in the back of the head with something hard, like maybe a piece of aluminum pool cage that blew down in the storm."

Hurricane Charley had wiped out virtually every one of the screened enclosures around the private swimming pools that were popular in the more affluent neighborhoods nearby. Jessie and Harry had scrounged some of these materials for their dock and probably left unused pieces lying around. I shook my head hard as if I could flick away the pictures that flashed through my mind.

Tiffany blew her nose again. "The cops have been asking weird questions—like where were we all day yesterday. How could they think me or Gordy would do something like that?" She dissolved into another round of sobs.

I touched her arm gently. Then she turned to me, and I held her like a baby, my own tears mixing with hers. When her sobs finally subsided, I tried to reassure her. "Both of you were at work all day, weren't you?" Seeing her nod, I said, "Then the police will know you couldn't have had anything to do with it."

"Yeah, the detective said they'd check it out." But she didn't sound reassured.

"Is there any word about Ben?"

Tiffany shook her head. Swiping at her cheeks, she stood up, walked over to the sink, and stared out the window. "They got divers out there looking . . . in the pond." Her voice broke. "That's why Gordy won't come home." She turned back to me. "But they also think he maybe ran away. They searched the boys' room again this morning, and they asked me to go through everything to see what was missing. Jessie's clothes were all there. But Ben took a lot more stuff than we knew about last night, even a couple dirty shirts and an extra pair of shoes." She twisted her tissue into a tight band around her fingers. "He took his stuffed animal too, the one he calls Floyd."

My throat tightened as I remembered the way Ben sometimes fiddled with the plush puppy's one white ear while he talked to me.

Tiffany's voice brought me back to the present. "And he must have took some cash. I know he had lawn-mowing money hid away somewhere—I don't know where. Guess he didn't trust us. The cops turned the place upside down looking for it, but they didn't find it."

"How much money?" I asked.

She thought a minute. "Sixty or seventy or eighty bucks, I guess. Maybe more." She turned back to the window, gazing out as she talked. "And those bastards kept asking us stuff like was Ben emotionally disturbed and did the boys fight a lot?"

A hard knot formed in my stomach. "What did you tell them?"

"I said of course they fight, they're brothers."

Tiffany came back to the couch and sank down. "That police detective, he wouldn't let it rest. He kept pumping me about when was the last time the boys had a real big fight, and I finally told him Ben bloodied Jessie's nose day before yesterday." She drew her knees up to her chest and hugged them. "It was a whopper of a fight, really, but of course I didn't say that. I don't even know what it was about."

Still, giving your brother a bloody nose was one thing. Smashing his head in was another. Ben would never do that. Never!

Would he?

As if reading my mind, Tiffany said, "I know me and Gordy are suspects. But the police also seem to be thinking maybe"—her voice dropped to a low whisper—"maybe Ben did it."

Chapter Eight

I left the Tollivers' trailer with my mind reeling. How could the police possibly suspect Ben of killing his brother? Unthinkable. Then again, if he didn't have anything to do with it, why did he run away?

There had to be some other explanation. He spent the night with a friend, some new acquaintance he hadn't told me about. Or—my mind was racing now—maybe Jessie's murderer killed him too. The police must have thought of that—why else would they be dragging the pond? But they hadn't found his body—not yet anyway. Tiffany would have known about it if they had. Could Ben have witnessed the murder, then run away? If so, maybe the police would find him unharmed.

As I rounded the corner, I felt myself drawn almost involuntarily to the scene at the Dalton Street Pond. I told myself to pass right on by; only ghouls haunted the scenes of tragedies like this. But my car turned left as if of its own volition.

I pulled in behind a line of parked cars and joined the ghouls who clustered near the outer circle of yellow crime scene tape. Beyond an inner ring, searchers plowed through the waist-high shore grass and bushes. Several figures in wet suits waded along the makeshift dock that stretched a short distance out over the shallow water. A dive team worked ten or twelve yards farther out. I shivered in spite of the warmth of the morning.

Against the yellow tape that kept the crowd at bay, Gordy Tolliver stood like a figure carved in stone. The curiosity seekers left a space around him. Maybe seeing him there made it too personal for them, or else they just didn't know what to say. I didn't know what to say either, but I made my way toward him. A tap on my shoulder stopped me. Whirling around, I stared into the breathless face of a seventy-ish woman in pink flowered shorts. "I recognize you," she puffed. "Seen you come by Tollivers' a lot of times. You DCF?"

"No, but I work with them pretty closely. I'm a Court Appointed Special Advocate for Ben and Jessie."

"Yeah, you got that official look. I'm Vera Mosely, across the street from Tollivers."

"Anna Sebastian. Now I know why you look familiar. I've seen you out in your yard picking up hurricane debris. You must be the only neighbor left on that end of the street."

"Huh. I had good sense I'd of left after the hurricane like the folks in the other side of my duplex. My place is still a mess." She swatted a mosquito on her blue-veined leg. "Guess you heard about the little boy," she said. Her thick glasses magnified her shocked round eyes.

I shuddered. "I still can't believe it."

"Me either. Pond ain't hardly big enough to fish in, but I seen that kid set out with a fishing pole after school nearly every day since Doug Grimm's widow gave him Doug's fishing gear—him and his buddy down the street. I thought the kids was a mite young to be out there alone, but weren't nothing I could do about it."

"Did Jessie's brother ever fish with him?"

"I can't see those boards where the kids fish—not from my house. But out walking, I seen the older boy over there with him once in a moon."

"You keep a pretty good watch on the neighborhood, don't you?."

"Honey, what else I got to do? My old man passed a year ago so it's just me rattling around over there."

"Did you see either of the Tolliver boys yesterday?"

"Cops asked me the same thing. The younger boy, Jessie, came hanging around the empty side of my duplex that morning. They go to school late, you know. Since the hurricane, the Punta Gorda kids all have to go to the high school up in Port Charlotte. I seen the kid there other mornings too way after the school bus left.

He'd just walk inside—the back screens are all blown out, you know, and the door glass too. Don't know what he found to do in there. But yesterday his dad hollered at him, and he high-tailed it home."

"What about Ben? Did you see him anytime?"

"The older brother? Not yesterday. He comes over there with Jessie once ever so often, but they don't play nice. The little boy usually ends up screaming."

Vera inched closer and cuffed her mouth with her hand as if to tell me a secret, but her voice resonated like a stage whisper. "I'm not surprised something bad happened, the way they act over at that trailer."

As heads turned toward us, I took Vera by the arm and led her away from the spectators. "What do you mean, 'the way they act'"?

"People coming all hours of the day and night." She swiped a strand of gray hair that had escaped its tight bun. "And that creep in the black BMW, I'm sure he's dealing."

My ears perked up. "What makes you think the creep is dealing?"

"Just the way he acts. They had an awful row when he came last Friday. Lots of yelling and screaming."

"Could you hear what they said?"

"What do you think I do, open my window and stick my head out?" For a moment Vera glared daggers; then before I could regroup, she punched me in the shoulder and let out a belly laugh. "Aw, Honey, I'm just the neighborhood busy-body, you know that. I didn't hear what they said, but I could tell she was scared. I could practically see her shake."

I glanced over my shoulder for Gordy, but I didn't see him now. Parked police vehicles obscured my view of the Tollivers' storm-ravaged duplex.

Vera lowered her voice. "They're still dragging for the body of the teenager."

I gazed out at the search teams, but all I could see in my mind's eye was Ben. I pictured his wavy blonde hair that hung down over his eyebrows, his haunted blue eyes, his thin face and dimpled chin, his full lips chapped from biting and licking, his even white teeth. He would grow into a handsome man if he ever learned to smile.

And if he wasn't floating somewhere on Dalton Street Pond.

Chapter Nine

On Sunday afternoon, I joined the mourners who streamed into the Methodist Church for Jessie's memorial service. The sanctuary had been stripped bare of carpet because of hurricane damage, and folding chairs replaced the traditional pews, but the place was packed. Jessie's murder and Ben's disappearance had hit all the local TV stations and the front page of the Charlotte *Sun*. The reports were vague about progress in the investigation, but everyone on both sides of the Peace River knew the time and place of the memorial service. Middle Schoolers, who had barely tolerated their different and difficult classmate in life, now poured out to pay their respects in death, bringing their parents along. Thankfully, the TV cameras were kept beyond the doors.

Scanning faces, I spotted the Owen family, all six of them. Rachel turned away as I approached, but her younger foster sister smiled at me. Candy swiped at red-rimmed eyes, and George stoically introduced their two new foster sons, who looked uncomfortable in their Sunday best. I wished them well. Two rows behind the Owens, Case Manager Melody Kahn waved. Sheila Quinn, our Guardian Ad Litem Coordinator, stepped into the aisle to give me a hug and motioned me to an empty chair two seats down from her.

Wearing an off-the-shoulder black dress that seemed more appropriate for a cocktail party, Tiffany Tolliver was escorted by an usher to the second row, followed by her husband, who looked like he had aged twenty years in the last three days. They slid into the second pew next to an obese older woman who reached behind Tiffany's back to pat Gordy's shoulder. Tiffany lurched forward, avoiding her touch. Was this a grandmother? If so, she would be Gordy's mother—I knew from reading the case files that Tiffany's mother was deceased. As Gordy covered the woman's hand with his, she glanced at him, revealing in profile a striking resemblance to him with her pointed nose and wide, forward-thrusting lower jaw. She had to be his mother. Interesting.

When the Tolliver family had first come to the attention of Child Protective Services, Gordy's mother was awarded custody of the boys, then ages six and nine. But after only a few months, she decided they were too difficult for her to handle and turned them over to DCF, thus condemning them to the foster care system. She'd had no further relationship with them or with their mother. But now, here she was. Death sometimes has a way of wiping slates clean.

I tried to block the whole memorial service from my mind—Jessie's grinning picture on the altar, the tear-jerking organ music, and the minister's empty words. "We know that in all things God works together for good for those who love Him," he intoned.

Balderdash! What kind of God would sit by and watch a pregnant woman consume enough alcohol to damage her unborn baby's brain? What kind of God would abandon children to a system that shuffled them through one foster home after another, then yanked them out of the best foster home they had ever known and handed them over to parents whose stability was largely untested?

I had fallen away from my family's fundamentalist church early in my relationship with Drew, when my dad started badgering me with biblical quotes about the evils of marrying a divorced man. But after I came to Florida without any family except a mother who no longer recognized me, loneliness prompted me to try out Peace River United Church in Port Charlotte. I was immediately drawn to its associate pastor, The Reverend Kate Alexander. In a congregation of mostly retired folk, she was close to my age. And like me, she was single. When she learned about my volunteer work with the Dependency Court, she asked me to help her start a program to assist foster families. Over time, we developed a close friendship. I couldn't imagine Kate suggesting that Jessie's tragic death had been part of God's plan!

Now, as I brought my wandering mind back to Jessie's memorial service, the minister was reciting the Twenty-Third Psalm. "The Lord is my shepherd; I shall not want."

Some shepherd! A line of Ben's first poem popped into my head. *The lamb is abandoned.* I turned the words over in my mind— first the Psalm, then Ben's poem. *The Lord is my shepherd. The lamb is abandoned.* The Lord is a shepherd who abandons a lamb? If that's what Ben's poem meant, he had turned the message of the Twenty-Third Psalm on its head!

When the service finally ended, I caught a glimpse of Ben's girlfriend rushing out into the church parking lot well ahead of her new foster brothers. I hurried toward her. "Rachel! May I talk to you a minute?"

Glancing back over her shoulder, she slowed but didn't stop. If one could look beyond the double nose piercing, the upper arm tattoo, and the chewing gum, Rachel was a beautiful girl. With her spiked black hair and big brown eyes, she didn't need the thick layer of mascara she insisted on wearing. She'd had some tough growing up years, and they showed. But I had watched her ease a young foster sister beyond the hurts of her past with sensitivity and compassion, and she had probably helped Ben more than a trained counselor could have.

She eyed me warily as I caught up with her. "I'm awfully worried about Ben," I panted. "The police think he ran away." Still walking, she tilted her head toward me as I plunged on. "Things disappeared from his room the same day Jessie was killed—things like clothes and your picture and the little stuffed dog he calls Floyd."

"Yeah, I know. Two of their goons grilled me for an hour yesterday, but I don't have any idea where he could be." With a defiant lift of her chin, she picked up her pace again.

Taken aback by her hostility, I wondered when I had become The Enemy. I thought I had established pretty good rapport with Rachel back when Ben lived with the Owens. I fell into step beside her. "Are you aware the police think Ben may have killed his brother?"

She skidded to a stop and gaped at me with what looked like genuine shock. "You're making that up, right?"

"I wish. The police know Ben and Jessie had a huge fight the day before Jessie was killed."

"Oh, that doesn't mean anything. They fought a lot." She began walking again. Following her gaze, I spotted the Owens' van several rows ahead.

I kept up with her. "You knew about the fight?"

The girl hesitated, then gave a small shrug. "Ben told me he gave his brother a black eye. He was feeling bad about it."

"What was the fight about?"

"Like I told the police, I don't know. But I do know Ben didn't kill his brother."

"What makes you so sure?"

Rachel stopped walking and looked me straight in the eye. "Ben wouldn't kill anyone, especially his brother. He just wouldn't."

"Maybe accidentally?"

"No." She shook her head vehemently.

"Then why did he run away?"

Rachel shrugged. "He hated living there." She started walking again.

"In the trailer?"

"With his mom and dad."

"Really?" Ben had never said anything like that to me.

"Really," she said. "Maybe that's why he ran away."

"Maybe. But to leave right after his brother was killed—the timing is a little spooky, don't you think?"

Rachel glared at me. "That doesn't prove anything."

"No," I said quickly. "No, it doesn't. And I'm not saying Ben had anything to do with Jessie's death. But whether he did or not, he's in a heap of trouble, Rachel. The police are combing the area for him, and they'll find him. He can't keep hiding. No matter what the problem is, even if he did . . . lose control of his temper or something"—I couldn't make myself say the words that jumped into my mind—"he's making things worse by running. You really don't have any idea where he is?"

"No, I told you that. No!"

"Well, if any thought comes to you or if you hear from him, please, *please* try to convince him to come in voluntarily. If he won't go to the police, ask him to call me. I'll help him, I promise. I'll find him a lawyer. We can all go to the police together."

"Like he ever in his life had a good experience with the police."

I didn't know the details of Ben's encounters with the law, but Rachel obviously did. One look at her face told me this beautiful young girl shared similar experiences—and the same emotions. "Still," I told her gently, "running away will only make his situation worse."

Rachel averted her gaze. "If Ben does contact me," she murmured, "I'll tell him what you said, but don't hold your breath."

The rest of the family had passed us, and the children were beginning the tumultuous process of boarding the Owens' van. Rachel started toward them. "One more thing, Rachel," I called.

She stopped a few feet from their Grand Caravan and waited for me with a put-upon sigh. "Did Ben ever mention anything about an assistant football coach named Jack Braxton?" I asked. "He's been giving Ben some special help."

For a fleeting instant, Rachel's eyes met mine, and I thought I read surprise in them. Then she gave her head a hard shake. "No, nothing." Turning away, she scurried into the van. I followed at a slower pace and gave Candy Owen a quick hug as she waited by the open vehicle. Before Rachel closed the sliding door with a resounding thunk, I heard her say, "Dad, could you drop me off at Jenny's house on the way home?"

A dozen questions hovered in my mind as I watched them drive off. Was Rachel telling me the truth, or did she really know something about Ben? Why had she suddenly become so unfriendly?

When I turned around, I came face to face with Gordon Tolliver. His eyes followed the departing van with obvious exasperation, but his expression brightened as I greeted him. "Oh, hi, Anna," he said. "I saw you talking to Ben's girlfriend. Did you by any chance ask if she knows where Ben could be?"

"Yes," I said wearily. "She doesn't."

His eyes narrowed as he glanced at the departing van. "So she says."

Chapter Ten

I came home from the memorial service with a ferocious headache and an aching heart. Downing two Tylenol, I stretched out on Mother's lumpy mattress and tried to nap, but my brain wouldn't shut up. Even quiet music on my IPod—my usual cure for insomnia—failed to calm the whirlwind in my mind. Why did Ben run away? Where could he be? He couldn't go far—not without transportation. Sure, he could hitch hike, but the police had put out an Amber Alert and his face was all over the newspapers, so who would pick him up? Tiffany said he took some money, but eighty dollars wouldn't get him very far. Why hadn't the police found him? What would happen to him if they did? Could he really have killed his brother?

No! He'd never do that! Not purposely anyway.

Accidentally?

Unwanted thoughts jammed my mind. Ben did lose his cool sometimes. His math teacher once told me he slugged a classmate for trying to swipe a piece of paper from him—a paper that turned out to be a poem Ben was writing.

Did Ben lose his temper with Jessie last Thursday? He was already angry with his brother because he wouldn't get on the school bus. He'd been upset enough to get a headache over it.

I knew Ben felt protective toward his brother. He always stood up for Jessie when other kids teased him. And he had turned down the opportunity to remain with several decent foster parents who couldn't cope with Jessie but offered to keep Ben. On the other hand, Ben did get terribly frustrated with his brother's irrational behavior. How many times had I had watched his jaw tighten when Jessie hit him! I had never seen Ben strike back, but Tiffany told me Ben sometimes "totally lost it," and he had drawn blood more than once.

Could Ben have gone out to the dock after his mom dropped him off last Thursday, maybe to have words with his brother about the school bus incident? Or maybe to continue the argument they'd had the day before, when Ben bloodied Jessie's nose? What if Jessie picked up one of the pieces of aluminum lying around their dock and lashed out at Ben? Jessie was capable of that. He wouldn't have understood the consequences. Maybe Ben tried to take it away from him and hit him with it as they struggled. Accidentally. Or maybe he was so frustrated he lost control of his temper. Maybe . . . maybe . . . maybe. I needed to stop thinking about all the maybes. But I couldn't.

I filled Mom's daisy-covered thermos—the good old glass-lined kind that would keep coffee hot all day long—and set it down at my computer station in the small office I had created out of her guest bedroom. From a cupboard below the bookshelf, I pulled out the thick brown file where I kept all my records on the Tolliver case.

One section of the case file held copies of my official reports to the judge, which I was required to turn in before every hearing. A quick review of these documents confirmed my recollection. All Ben's school counselors and teachers—even the wonderful English teacher who gave him A's—told me they believed he had emotional problems that were serious enough to warrant professional counseling.

My first report for the court noted that Candy Owen had taken Ben for a psychological evaluation soon after he moved in. His therapist observed that Ben refused to meet her eyes. In the absence of indications of autism, she labeled this a "low self-esteem problem." She also suspected Post Traumatic Stress Syndrome, although she couldn't identify specific past traumas because Ben answered her questions in monosyllables. She recommended medication and continued therapy, but Ben flatly refused both. Candy and George decided to honor his wishes.

My latest report for the judge mentioned Ben's English teacher's concern because his grades had dropped since the hurricane. I had quoted her at some length.

Our school is experiencing a rash of similar problems. With so many children uprooted from their homes, whole families are living with friends and relatives who don't have room for them. Adding all the students from the Punta Gorda high school into this school adds turbulence. We are all struggling. But I am especially concerned about Ben. He is bright, talented, and sensitive. And this is only the latest of many upheavals in his life. He seems unusually moody and withdrawn. I really think he needs psychological counseling.

Ben had reluctantly agreed to give counseling a try with a different therapist, and my report pleaded for a new psychiatric evaluation. The judge ordered it, but the process of obtaining the necessary financial assistance seemed to have run into terminal snags.

Refilling my coffee mug from the thermos, I browbeat myself with accusations. I should have fought harder for counseling for Ben. I should have nagged his DCF case manager Melody Kahn every three days. I guess I just didn't realize how bad his problems were. I had developed good rapport with Ben, so he probably behaved differently with me than he did in other parts of his life. I should have listened to his teachers.

And I should have paid more attention to his poetry. I turned to the section of the case file labeled "Correspondence etc." and reread the first poem he had given me, *The Dark*. The title was appropriate—the poem was so black it should have scared me. Instead I had praised him for his talent. How could I have missed the pain of his inner world? *Night comes like a tiger, relentless and silent, stalking its prey.* That went way beyond a normal fear of the dark! *Whispers in darkness, secrets behind closed doors never heard in the light.* What terrible secrets was he keeping in his young mind? What had he been ordered never to reveal?

Dreams in dark bedrooms—white bread and tuna. Reach out with hope. Wake to the nightmare. That must refer to times when he went to bed hungry and dreamed of food, only to wake to the "nightmare" of empty cupboards.

About the rest of the poem, I had absolutely no clue. *The serpent bares its fangs and slithers over the stones.* What in God's name could that mean? *Wrath stomps on mercy.* Wrath? That had a biblical ring, didn't it? When had Ben learned to use words like "wrath"? *The dogs howl, break down the gates.* More symbolic imagery. *The lamb is abandoned, the angel forsaken. The Dark overcomes.* Again, that biblical ring.

My thoughts flashed to Jessie's memorial service this morning and the minister's reading of the Twenty-Third Psalm. "The Lord is my shepherd." Not in Ben's world! In Ben's world, lambs were abandoned!

Taking another swig of coffee, I savored its bitter heat. The biblical imagery puzzled me. Tiffany and Gordy weren't church goers. The Owens were Presbyterians, but Ben refused to go to Sunday School and his foster parents had never forced the issue. Yet this poem had a clear religious overtone.

I got out *First Down,* Ben's second poem. I was struck by the radical difference between it and his earlier poem. No opaque symbolism here. This was a straightforward story about a young man who hated football and hated his dad for making him play until a coach came along and showed him how to catch a ball. The joy of completing a pass and making a first down. Nothing obscure about this poem. Nothing dark either—except the poignant wish that his mother had come to watch

Glancing back at his first poem, *The Dark,* I wished I could make sense out of it. What could that line about the serpent mean? Who were the howling dogs? Was Ben the abandoned lamb and the forsaken angel? Or did these images refer to Jessie? Could the answers to these questions possibly hold clues to what happened Thursday night? Probably not. I mean, really, how could they? Still I couldn't get the questions out of my mind.

I picked up the phone and called the one person I thought might be able to come up with answers—my friend and pastor, Kate Alexander. Even if she couldn't answer my questions, a visit with Kate would almost certainly lift my spirits. Truth was, I was starting to feel overcome by darkness myself.

Chapter Eleven

An hour later I sat at Kate's kitchen table, devouring leftovers from Friday night's potluck dinner. "Ummm, meatloaf, spaghetti, and lime Jell-O. Just what I needed," I said. "I'm in the pits."

"Because?"

That was one of the things I liked about Kate. She listened between the lines. I looked into her smiling brown eyes and tried to think how to begin. I decided on a question. "Have you read in the news about the boy who was murdered and his brother who is missing?" When her expression turned serious, I added, "I'm their Guardian Ad Litem."

Kate let out an audible breath and ran her fingers through her cropped black hair. She wasn't exactly pretty, but there was something in the lines of her face and the lights in her eyes that drew me to her. "No wonder you're in the pits," she said. "I read in yesterday's paper that the older brother may be a suspect?"

"Yes, and I keep asking myself if I could have done something to keep this from happening."

Kate cocked her head at me. "And how exactly would you have done this magical 'something'?"

"I'm not supposed to talk about my cases," I said, ignoring her light tone.

"I know. But as of this moment, you are having a counseling session with your pastor, and I am bound by professional ethics never to repeat what you tell me. I sense that this case has you tied in knots."

A heaviness suddenly lifted from my shoulders, making me realize just how alone I'd been feeling. "I'm kicking myself all over the place because I haven't been able to get counseling for Ben. I knew he needed it. I even got the judge to order it, but it never happened. I should have tried to help him find them find a way to pay for it."

Kate focused on her meatloaf, giving me space. After awhile, I went on. "And I should have asked him more questions about a poem he wrote. Now, when it's too late, I realize it was a cry for help, but I didn't pick up on it. Instead of trying to find out what it meant, I just told him how much talent he had. Now I'm wondering if I should give his poetry to the police, but I'm not sure it's a good idea."

She stopped eating. "You think something in the poem could help the police?"

"Maybe I'm reading too much into it, but his poem titled *The Dark* talks about 'secrets behind closed doors.' And it's filled with strange images—a serpent that shows its fangs, dogs that howl and break down gates, and a lamb that's abandoned. It's like there are things Ben needs to get off his chest, but they're too awful—or too secret—for him to say straight out, so he uses symbols instead. And I might be wrong, but I think some of the language he uses comes from the Bible." Handing her a copy I'd made of *The Dark*, I told her, "Ben wrote this about two months ago."

Furrows formed in her brow as she read. "I sure see why you told him he has talent," she said after she finished. "How do you think this poem could help the police?"

I hesitated, wondering if she'd think I'd read too many mystery stories, but she waited expectantly, so I continued. "I keep thinking about howling dogs and slithering serpents. Both of Ben's parents have a history of substance abuse. They claim they've turned their lives around, and their random drug screens have all come up clean, but the pros know ways to cheat the test. And one of their neighbors saw a guy in a black BMW stop at their trailer and get in a screaming fight with Ben's mom. The neighbor thought the guy was a dealer. I'm wondering if the dogs and serpents could refer to the drug scene. Maybe if the police read the poem, they'd be more inclined to look beyond the family for suspects."

"So why not give it to them?"

"I'm afraid they'll use it as evidence that Ben is emotionally disturbed. Do you think he sounds troubled enough to kill his brother?"

Kate studied the poem for several minutes. "I think he sounds angry. And maybe depressed."

I waited for her to go on.

"I'm sure you're right about the religious imagery. *Wrath* and *lamb* and *angel* aren't kids' words. Someone in his past must have taught Ben a whole lot about the Bible. He probably paid pretty close attention; otherwise he wouldn't remember it so well. I'm betting he was a pretty pious kid during some period of his growing up. But wrath doesn't stomp on mercy. Lambs aren't abandoned, and angels aren't forsaken." As she spoke, she underlined the words with her index fingers. "Not in my Bible, they're not."

"So . . . ?"

"So he was probably told that God protects the faithful the way shepherds care for their lambs. And that angels watch over them."

"Then he and Jessie got yanked away from their parents—and who knows what happened to them in some of those foster homes they lived in. And God didn't help them."

"Very likely," Kate said with a nod. "So in his poetry, Ben throws all those grand promises right back in God's face."

"You think he's angry at God?"

Kate pursed her lips in concentration. "Yes, but not just at God. His whole poem is filled with venomous images like the slithering serpent and howling dogs. I have a hunch he's very, very angry about a lot of things. He probably can't admit how furious he is, so he buries his feelings—or disguises them in obscure imagery. The trouble is, buried anger often turns inward where it can fester up into a huge guilt complex. All kids tend to think everything is about them, you know, so they hold themselves responsible for stuff that isn't even remotely their fault. I can't begin to guess what secrets Ben is hiding, but I get a strong feeling he doesn't like himself very well. The whole tone of his poem shouts despair. Especially the last stanza: *The lamb is abandoned, the angel forsaken. The Dark overcomes.*"

I struggled to take in what she was saying. Could Ben possibly feel responsible for some of the dark secrets that could never be told in the light? Could that be why he hardly ever looked anyone straight in the eyes? His therapist thought so. She called it a self-esteem problem. "You could be right," I said slowly, "about him not liking himself very well. And about burying his anger. And about despair. "

Silence settled glumly over us. "Still," Kate said finally, "anger isn't a criminal offense. And I don't see any indication that Ben's fury was directed at his brother. If Jessie is anywhere in this poem, he's the forsaken angel or the abandoned lamb. So why not give the poem to the police? Your thought about dogs and snakes representing the drug scene could give them something new to think about."

"I suppose."

"What's bothering you?" Kate asked, peering at me as if she could glimpse the tsunami going on in my head.

I pulled a copy of *First Down* from my purse and handed it to her. "Ben gave me this poem the day before Jessie was murdered. If I give the police *The Dark*, I should give them this one too."

Kate read it quickly. "This sure is different from the first poem! So upbeat—a success story. What changed?"

I took a deep breath before I answered. "A coach named Jack Braxton."

Propping an elbow on the table, she rested her chin in her hand. I sensed the vibration of her counselor's antenna as she peered over her knuckles at me. "Tell me about this coach."

I spilled out the whole story—how Jack had singled Ben out for individual coaching, how much Ben had improved, and finally how Jack and I had begun dating. "He's out of town now," I told her. "He got called to Nebraska for his aunt's funeral." I couldn't meet her gaze as I added, "Actually, he left the day Jessie was murdered."

"Have you heard from him since?" she asked sharply.

"No, but he said he might be away for awhile, tending to his aunt's estate. Still—." I wanted Kate to say something to save me from facing my worst nightmare, but she didn't. When the silence began to bug me, I said, "I know the timing is pretty eerie. But Jack seems like such a good guy, making time in his life to work with kids and all. And he's helped Ben so much."

Kate still rested her chin in her hand, and her index finger made tiny circles on her cheekbone. Finally she said, "I feel obligated to mention that pedophiles often volunteer in youth programs, and they become skilled at winning the trust of vulnerable young people." She must have read the horror on my face because she quickly added, "But to coach in the Pop Warner leagues, Jack would have been required to pass a background check. I think they're pretty strict about that."

I grasped at the straw of hope. "Then if there was something awful in his past, the background check would have turned it up." I felt her gaze on me. "Probably would have," I amended. "But—"

"But you're thinking?" Kate asked quietly.

"I'm thinking I really don't know Jack very well."

Chapter Twelve

The next day, Monday, two unpleasant tasks stared me in the face. The first was to call on Rachel York. I couldn't get yesterday's conversation with Ben's girlfriend out of my mind. She'd seemed so hostile. Nervous. Evasive. And when I asked if Ben had ever mentioned Coach Jack, I thought I'd read shock on her face. Or panic. Was it my imagination, or did she know something about Ben that involved Jack? I'd once had a decent relationship with Rachel. Maybe if I confronted her on her own turf, I could worm something more out of her.

My second unpleasant task was to stop by the Punta Gorda Police Station to give both of Ben's poems to one of the detectives working the Tolliver case. I needed to let them know that Coach Jack Braxton had taken a special interest in the young poet and to tell them Jack had "left town" the same day Jessie was murdered. If Jack's story checked out . . . . Surely it would. And then I could stop worrying about it. But if it didn't? I shuddered.

I timed my visit with Rachel for four o'clock, hoping she would be home from school by then. As I crossed the bridge into Punta Gorda and turned right onto Virginia, I realized that my knuckles were white on the steering wheel. Was I actually nervous about talking with this fourteen-year-old girl? Yes. What if I couldn't break through her sudden hostility? Worse yet, what if I did? What if she told me something I really didn't want to hear?

The Owens lived in Punta Gorda's historic district, where homes ranged from upscale restorations to handyman specials. Candy and George's four-bedroom fell about half way in between. Hurricane Charley had left its devastation here in seemingly arbitrary patterns, whipping up one house as if with a gigantic electric beater, yet sparing the place right next door. The yellow and brown frame where Ben and Jessie had lived for ten months and where Rachel still resided was one of the lucky ones. Only the ever-present blue tarp on the roof and the stump of what had been a huge live oak tree in the front yard gave evidence of the horrific storm that had created so much havoc up and down the street.

Candy Owen opened the door at my first knock. To my surprise, her usually sunny face was drawn and blotchy, and her eyes brimmed with tears. Wrapping me in her arms, she pulled me tight against her soft bosom, and I felt her body shake with sobs. "Oh, Anna, you heard," she said as I broke away. "Thanks for coming."

"Heard what?" Somehow I realized I didn't want to know the answer

"About Rachel."

I shook my head, anxiety cramping my belly.

"She's run away."

"Run away?" My ears took in the words, but my mind refused to grasp them.

"This morning." She led me into her comfortable living room and closed the front door behind us. "She was here at breakfast, but I'm still driving our new boys to school, so I left before she did. Then I went on to do my volunteer stint at the library. When I got home around noon, I found her note."

"A note! What did it say?"

"The police took it, but I remember every word. 'Dear Mom and Dad, I'm going to join Ben to try to talk him into giving himself up. I'll call when I can. I love you.'" On this last line, her voice broke. "It's the first time Rachel ever actually said, 'I love you.'" A fresh spasm of sobs overtook her.

Taking her gently by the arm, I led her to the couch and sat down beside her. A fireball of emotions burst over me. Fear, anger, and yes, relief. "It must mean they're both safe," I said.

Candy's tears subsided a bit, and she reached into the pocket of her shorts for a wadded tissue. "But it sounds like Ben really did kill his brother."

"Or at least Rachel thinks he did. She may not know for sure." Grasping at every shred of hope I could find, I added, "Even if he did, he couldn't have done it on purpose."

"No, of course not." Her eyes flashed for a moment; then the spark faded and she shook her head darkly. "But God knows what the police will make out of it."

"He's got to turn himself in, Candy. No matter what he's done, he's making his situation worse by running. Maybe Rachel can persuade him." My thoughts returned to yesterday afternoon and the shock on the girl's face when I'd asked about Jack. "Did Rachel ever mention anything about a football coach named Jack?"

She frowned. "Not that I recall. Why?"

"I'm trying to think of anyone Ben trusted, anyone he could possibly have turned to for help. Coach Jack had been giving him special attention." Replaying the encounter with Ben's girlfriend in my mind, I had another flash of memory. "I heard Rachel ask George to take her to Jenny's house yesterday after the memorial service."

Candy nodded. "Jenny's her best friend." Studying me through red-rimmed eyes, she added, "Ben isn't there, if that's what you're thinking. The police have searched the whole place, and they're watching the house."

"Still," I said, "Rachel must know how to contact Ben; otherwise how could she join him? I wonder if Jenny could be helping them somehow—maybe letting them use her phone or a computer."

Candy's face brightened. "Good thought! I don't know if the police checked that out, but I'll call right now and ask."

"I'm on my way to talk to them. I'll mention it too."

"Ask for one of the detectives who were here this morning—Underwood or Domagala."

"OK. Thanks."

Sick at heart, I turned up Virginia toward the police station. As I waited for the stoplight at Taylor, my cell phone chimed. I had no intention of answering it, but I picked it up to read the Caller ID. *John Braxton*!!! I pushed the *talk* button.

"Anna," came the familiar voice. "It's Jack. I'm home, and I just read my morning paper. I'm reeling from shock."

From behind me, an irritated honk announced that the light had turned green. "Hold on a second; I'm in a bunch of traffic. I'll pull off."

I turned right on Taylor and ducked into an empty parking spot. "Are you still there?"

"Still here—in body at least. But I can't believe it. Jessie Tolliver was murdered and Ben has disappeared?"

"It's true, Jack." My heart pounded in my ears. After the God-awful thoughts I'd been having about him, here he was, back home like he said he would be. And sounding normal as chicken soup. Shocked, of course. Aghast even. In other words normal, given the circumstances.

"And the police suspect Ben?"

"Yes, and you haven't heard the latest. His girlfriend, Rachel, ran away to join him this morning. She left a note saying she was going to try to talk him into giving himself up." He was quiet so long I thought he'd dropped off the line. "Jack?"

"Yeah." He sounded very subdued. "I'm having a rough time absorbing it all."

"I know." I felt all my suspicions melt away. Jack hadn't disappeared into thin air; he'd been at his aunt's funeral for the last four days, just like he'd said. Relief washed over me. "How was your trip?"

"All right, as those things go."

"Guess you didn't have to stay a long time to take care of things."

"No, it turned out I didn't have too much work to do. But the reason I called is . . . I was wondering if we could still have that dinner date I had to break last Thursday?"

"Well . . . I guess we could."

"I'm cooking up a pot of spaghetti. Why don't you come help me eat it?"

"Tonight?" I checked my watch. Five o'clock.

"You have to eat somewhere," he added persuasively. "And I make a mean spaghetti sauce." I could hear the smile in his voice. "A huge queen palm fell across my driveway and the curbs are stacked high with yard trash, so parking and getting around over here is a bit tricky. I'll pick you up. How about six o'clock?"

Six! Yikes! That left no time to go the police, but I was already rethinking what I needed to tell them about Jack anyway. He sounded casual and relaxed. If he'd had anything to do with Ben's disappearance, he certainly wouldn't invite me for dinner. Would he?

"OK," I said, and I felt my spirits lift.

Chapter Thirteen

As Jack pulled into a grassy vacant lot a block from his house an hour and a half later, I understood what he meant when he said parking and getting around was tricky. In some places, the yard trash that littered the curbs was higher than our heads. "We'll have to walk from here," he explained as he locked up the car. "I had to drive across the front lawn to get my car around the queen palm that fell across the drive, and it's not an exercise I want to repeat."

Jack had greeted me with a big smile, and I'd felt foolishly glad to see him. Now as I took his arm while we traipsed over the uneven ground, I felt some of the strain of the past few days drain out of me. No, I didn't know him very well, but walking beside him, listening to his easy chitchat, I could not possibly picture him as a pedophile. In spite of Kate's warning.

"Watch out for fire ants," he cautioned.

"I am!" I'd lived in this part of Florida long enough to be wary of those nasty little creatures. They sent an army up the feet and legs of anyone who disturbed their large gray nests, leaving a patch of itchy, pus-filled blisters behind them.

As we rounded the corner onto Jack's street, I let out a small gasp as I saw how hard Charley had hit his neighborhood. Next door to Jack was a blown-out house with exposed rafters and the letters R.O.E. spray-painted on its garage door. These initials, I had learned, stood for Right of Entry and authorized insurance adjusters, contractors, and demolition workers to enter. Jack's place, a light green concrete block, appeared basically intact although a front window was boarded up and the roof was covered by the ubiquitous blue tarp. "Looks like the storm broke a window," I commented.

"Yeah. A piece of the neighbor's roof tile sailed right through it. It's the only one that got broken, thank God." As we made our way around the fallen palm to the front door, Jack added, "If you think this is bad, you should see the grapefruit tree that bit the dust in my back yard."

Inside, the house was moderately cluttered and lacked a woman's touch. In the combination living/dining room, vertical blinds covered a large window, and a few paintings hung at assorted heights. There were no curtains or photographs—nothing that looked personal. A small, no-frills kitchen opened onto an enclosed back porch, where the only table was covered with computers in various stages of decomposition.

The house smelled marvelous, and I was suddenly hungry. As I leaned against the sink watching Jack pop a handful of spaghetti into a boiling pot, I commented, "You look very at home in the kitchen."

He grinned. "Before I got married, I learned to cook to keep from starving. Afterwards"—the smile faded—"Heather conned me by telling me lies about what a magic touch I had in the kitchen." The smile returned. "Now, I find it relaxing. And of course, I don't have much choice. I can't stand a steady diet of restaurant food."

Changing the subject, I asked, "What made you decide to coach Pop Warner football?"

He forked out a string of spaghetti and tasted it. "Couple more minutes to go," he said, pulling a loaf of bread from the oven and cutting large, tempting slices. Glancing up from his work, he answered my question. "I thought it was time to stop moping and do something constructive. And I like football. I played in high school until I decided I was going to get killed if I kept on." With a good-natured shrug he added, "When the guys I tackled kept dragging me along as if I wasn't there, I had to admit I'm not built for the sport." He gave the sauce a stir.

"You've done some coaching through the years though, haven't you?" When he studied me quizzically, I added, "You're so good with the boys."

Jack tested the spaghetti again, declared it done, and drained it. "Yeah, I've done some." He served us each a bountiful helping, reached into the fridge for salads, and set our feast out on the dining table at the end that wasn't covered with computer parts. He offered me a chair and sat down across the corner from me.

Diving into my food, I oohed and ahed over the pasta, which was, in truth, fantastic. Obviously pleased, he divulged his secrets—fresh basil and a spoonful of barbeque sauce. Then we lapsed into silence. Were we going to go on all evening avoiding the painful subject that must be at the front of both our minds?

As if reading my thoughts, Jack said, "I feel awful about Ben. Jessie too, though I didn't really know him." He set his fork down. "I've read the newspapers, of course, but I'm anxious to hear your version of what happened."

As I summarized the events of the past four days, Jack's face grew somber. "And now his girlfriend has run away to join him?" he asked, repeating my words as if he couldn't quite believe them. "Do you know anything more about that?"

"She left a note. Said she was going to try to talk him into turning himself in."

"Let's hope she can do it."

"She has a better chance than anyone else, I think."

"Yeah." He finished the last bite on his plate and chewed contemplatively.

After I'd eaten all I could, I got up, collected my purse from the kitchen, and pulled a folded sheet of paper from it. "I brought a copy of one of Ben's poems. He said he didn't mind if you read it. Of course, he tried to act very nonchalant, but I think he was pleased you were interested."

I pushed *First Down* across the table to him. He took a very long time reading it and cleared his throat a couple times. I sipped my iced tea and focused on the painting of a woodland scene that hung crookedly on the wall. After a few minutes, he leaned forward with one elbow on the table. "Don't you have any idea where those two kids could be?"

"No, I really don't. I've thought and thought about them."

"You know Ben's friends, don't you? Can't you think of anyone the police might not have checked?" His gaze was intense.

I shook my head. "He's pretty much of a loner, Jack. I can't name a single buddy except maybe Harry Nagorski down the street, and he's Jessie's age."

"What about Ben's girlfriend? She must have friends."

"Oh, she does. Lots of them, both boys and girls. I don't know any of their names except her best friend Jenny, but the police are checking out everyone that Rachel hung out with."

Frowning, he pushed a stray strand of spaghetti absently around his plate with his fork. "You said Rachel left a note saying she was going to try to talk Ben into giving himself up?" When I nodded, he said, "So that must mean she knew where he was. How else could she meet him?"

My mind drifted back to yesterday afternoon when I'd caught up with Rachel after Jessie's memorial service. When I looked up, I found Jack staring at me.

"Did you think of something?" he asked.

I told him about my attempt to talk with Rachel. "She seemed nervous," I added. "And when she got into the family van, I overheard her ask her foster dad to drop her off at her friend Jenny's house." I paused, turning that over in my mind. Jack still watched me intently.

"I can't believe Jenny's parents would let Ben stay there," I continued. "In fact Candy Owen, Rachel's foster mom, told me the police are keeping an eye on that house, so Ben definitely isn't there. But I wonder if Jenny might be letting Rachel contact Ben somehow." I searched Jack's eyes. He hadn't moved a muscle since I began my story. I went on, thinking out loud. "I'm sure the police are monitoring Jenny's phone, but what about email?"

"Email," Jack echoed softly. "Have you mentioned this to anyone?"

It seemed an odd question. "I told Candy about it, and she promised to call the police right away to ask if they'd checked out Jenny's computer."

Jack's face had become an expressionless mask. "When was that?" His hand gripped the edge of the table.

"This afternoon. Just before you called, actually. Why?"

"Just curious."

Abruptly, he slid his chair back, screeching it against the floor tile, and stood up. "Excuse me a minute, will you Anna?" Without waiting for a response, he added. "Your comment about email reminded me I'm expecting an important one from a customer this evening." Suddenly he was talking very fast. "It's about a big computer job that's supposed to come in tomorrow. The coffee's made; help yourself. I'll be right back." With that, he fairly sprinted toward a hallway that surely led to the bedrooms.

Nonplussed, I watched his back disappear. This high strung, fast-talking Jack seemed a different person from the relaxed, confident football coach I thought I knew. I was suddenly afraid. Why was a job for tomorrow such a sudden emergency? Why couldn't it wait until after I left? All of Kate's warnings about men who seem extraordinarily adept at gaining the trust of vulnerable youth surged back into my mind.

I started toward the coffee pot, then changed my mind. I was keyed up enough without adding caffeine. Indecisively, I ambled to the doorway that led from the living/dining room into a short, well-lighted hallway. I counted four doors, three of them open. The closed one was probably a closet—not enough wall space for anything bigger. One of the open doors would be a bathroom. The other two surely were bedrooms. A light shone through the one on the left. I took a step toward it. Stopped. Then, my heart pounding, I moved resolutely down the hall.

Chapter Fourteen

In the crowded space between the wall and the foot of a queen-sized bed, Jack hunched at a makeshift computer station—two card tables and a wooden dining room chair. His back was to me.

As I eased into the room, he shifted in his chair, and I took a step backward. A split second later, he turned and saw me.

"Hi," I said with forced casualness. "I came down to use your bathroom and saw your light."

"Be my guest," he said. "I'll only be a couple more minutes." He turned back to his computer.

I retreated with full intentions of returning to the dining area. But as I glanced into the room across the hall, I spotted a good-sized computer station and an upholstered desk chair. Odd. Why did Jack squeeze all his electronics into a corner of his bedroom while this comfortable work area sat empty?

Pausing in the doorway, I glanced around the room. In the illumination from the hall, I saw that it had only one window—the boarded up one I'd noticed on my way into the house. The room was crammed with furniture. Under the damaged window, two filing cabinets and a narrow bookshelf filled the space next to the computer station. On the adjoining wall, a long table—the kind one might find in a church basement—was wedged between a file cabinet and the head end of a bare rollaway bed, whose length extended to within an inch of the doorway where I stood. Like the computer work station, the table top was clear. In fact, the whole room was immaculate—much cleaner than the rest of the house. And the walls were bare except for something framed that hung over the bed. A family photo?

Overcome with curiosity, I tiptoed into the room to see what it was. Very, very stupid move! Because my left toe caught on the metal foot of the rollaway! Before I knew what happened, I found myself unceremoniously draped over the foot of the bed, frantically trying to brace myself on the flimsy mattress as it slid halfway off its frame.

Panicked, I managed to regain my equilibrium and stand up. Had Jack heard me? I didn't think I'd made much noise. I listened a moment. Heard nothing. No telltale screech of a chair sliding. No footsteps. Quietly, I reached down to slide the mattress back to its original position. And stopped. There was something on top of the bed's metal springs. A sheet of paper. I stared at it a moment before my brain processed what I was seeing. My insides turned to ice when I took in the familiar boyish scrawl. *FORSAKEN ANGEL by Ben Tolliver.*

Suddenly I remembered Ben telling me he always hid his poems under his mattress so no one would read them.

Ben had been here, sleeping in this bed!

I grabbed the poem, shoved the mattress back the way I'd found it, and bolted for the bathroom. Stuffing the poem into my bra, I flushed the toilet, ran water in the sink for a moment, then ordered myself to walk calmly out into the hall.

I nearly collided with Jack.

He let out a startled "Oh!" Collecting himself, he said hastily, "Something has come up about the job I have to do tomorrow." Taking my arm, he propelled me toward the dining area, turning out lights as we walked. "I better get you home." He flicked another switch, plunging the whole house into darkness. "We'll go out the back door," he told me as we neared the end of the hall. "It's closer to the car."

"Just let me grab my purse." I tried to sound casual, as if I thought his behavior was perfectly normal. "I left it on one of the dining room chairs. Could you turn on a light?"

"We can pick it up on the way out. Here, take my arm. I'll guide you."

OK, this was definitely weird. And it got weirder a moment later when the doorbell rang.

Before I could react, Jack flattened me against his chest, clamping his hand over my mouth. His other arm pinned my body like a vise. "Don't make a sound," he hissed. As if I could even breathe.

The doorbell rang more insistently. Then came a loud knock. A shout. "Punta Gorda Police! Anybody home?" I heard the rattle of a doorknob and more pounding.

"We're not here," Jack whispered in my ear. "They won't break in unless they have a warrant. Don't make a sound, understand? I don't want to hurt you." Slowly but relentlessly he dragged me backwards into the hall.

Chapter Fifteen

Jack pressed his hand over my mouth and nose, smothering the scream that formed in my throat. "Don't make a sound," he hissed.

I'm going to pass out, I thought. But just as my head began to spin, he lowered his fingers, uncovering my nose. "I can't breathe," I mumbled into his palm.

"Yes you can. Stop fighting it. Breathe through your nose."

I focused on the simple challenge of taking air into my lungs. In out, in out. He was right; I could do it. For what seemed an eternity, he crushed me against his body, not speaking, not moving, and not loosening his vise-like pressure. I felt the pounding of his heart against my back.

The doorbell again. Three times, four. Before I could let out the blood-curdling scream I was planning, Jack covered my nose again.

"Be quiet," he hissed. "I don't want to hurt you."

Yeah, right.

The doorbell kept ringing—five, six, seven times. Jack backed deeper into the hallway, dragging me with him. We stood there, a caricature of lovers, until at last the knocking stopped. The doorbell grew mute and the male voices faded. A few minutes later, I heard a car engine start. The police were leaving. I'd missed my chance.

The ringing of the telephone split the silence. Jack tightened his hold on me as I counted four rings. From the bedroom came the sound of his voice, cheerful and upbeat. His answering machine. I half expected it to be the cops, but it wasn't. It was Mike Peterson, Ben and Jessie's coach. "I hate to bug you," said the recorded voice, "but Pop Warner says they haven't received your background check yet. Please turn it in ASAP. I need you bad, but I can't let you coach again till they give me the OK."

"Guess that's not going to happen," Jack muttered in my ear as he wrestled me down the hall and into the doorway of the room where I had found Ben's poem. Before I could collect my thoughts, he gave me a shove that landed me half way across the floor. As I scrambled to my feet, the pocket door closed. Before I could get to it, I heard a soft pounding just outside it. Grabbing its small latch, I pulled with all my might. The door squeaked, but it would not open. Jack must have jammed something between it and the frame to keep it from sliding! I heard more pounding as I continued to tug on the latch.

"Sorry, Anna," Jack said through the door. "I don't want to talk to the police right now, and I don't have time to explain. Some of them may still be watching the house, so I need to slip out the back door, and I can't let you stop me."

I screamed names at him that rarely escaped my lips.

"You'll be OK. The police are sure to come back with a warrant before long"

I pressed both my palms against the door and struggled with all my strength to work it free. If I could just get it open enough to slip my fingers around its edge, I might make progress. But I couldn't.

When I took a moment to rest, I heard muffled noises that seemed to come from across the hall. With one ear pressed to the jammed door, I concluded that Jack was opening and closing dresser drawers. After what felt like five or ten minutes, I heard footsteps pad down the hall and fade away. I pounded on the door and screamed—an exercise in futility. Finally, I collapsed against the door, exhausted. I listened for running feet, shouts, gunshots, sirens—any sign that the police had spotted Jack as he made his escape. In some distant part of the house, a clock struck. I counted the chimes. Eleven.

Then silence.

Chapter Sixteen

I pounded on the door in bone- scorching, gut-burning, fire-breathing fury. How could Jack have done this to me? I trusted him! How could I have been so stupid? I switched from banging on the door to tugging on the metal plate that served as both latch and handle. Nothing budged.

Giving up on the door for the moment, I turned toward the room's only window. No light shone through the plywood that covered it from the outside. Hurricane damage, Jack had said. More likely he'd nailed it shut to keep Ben locked up here.

Touching the poem that was still in my bra, I finally got the picture. A clear but very ugly picture. Jack hadn't gone to Nebraska; he'd been here all the time, keeping Ben prisoner. He'd converted his office into a prison, cramming in a rollaway bed. Now I was trapped in the same room where he'd held Ben. And my cell phone was in my purse, which I'd left at the table. My fury was quickly turning to panic. I had to get a grip on myself.

I struggled with the door until my fingers ached and my knees trembled with fatigue. I couldn't move it even a quarter inch. What about the window? If any of the police were still watching the house, I should try to get their attention. Feeling my way in the darkness, I climbed up onto the two-drawer filing cabinets. Pressing my palms against the wall for balance, I stood up and cautiously felt for jagged edges. Although the plywood covered the whole window, the lower pane felt intact. Working my fingers upward, I discovered that the glass had been removed from the upper pane. I pounded on the plywood and hollered. After a few minutes, I stopped to listen. Nothing.

I climbed down and opened up all the desk drawers, exploring them by touch, hoping to find something heavy that I could use to pound against the plywood. I found paper and pencil. Nothing else.

Returning to the door, I tugged until my fingers bled and my back screamed. Sweat ran down my forehead even though the room wasn't overly warm. Discouraged, I sank down on the rollaway bed to rest.

Where was Ben now? Could he still be somewhere in this house, gagged and bound? Surely not. Jack wouldn't have invited me here if he'd been holding Ben captive, would he? Then did Jack kill him? After he . . . got finished with him? But Rachel's note said she was running away to try to talk Ben into giving himself up. That meant he was alive, didn't it? At least Rachel thought he was. So maybe Ben managed to escape from Jack's house somehow.

I climbed back up onto the filing cabinets and hammered on the plywood again, shouting until my voice gave out. Then I spent more fruitless time trying to work the door open.

The last hours replayed in my mind in an endless loop. How could Jack have known the police were coming? We'd been pleasantly chatting at the table when he suddenly dashed to his bedroom like a madman. What set him off?

We'd been discussing where Ben could be. I'd told him about talking with Rachel after Jessie's memorial service yesterday afternoon and about my hunch that she might know more than she would admit about where Ben was. I mentioned that I'd overheard her ask her foster dad to drop her at Jenny's house on the way home. I'd wondered aloud if she was using her friend's computer to email Ben. Jack had repeated the word "email" as if I'd spoken a revelation from on high. Then he had turned into someone I didn't know.

"*Did you mention this to anyone?*" he'd asked me. I remembered how his hands had gripped the edge of the table. But I'd been clueless. I admitted I'd told Candy Owen just hours ago, and she'd promised to call the police about it right away. That's when Jack took off down the hall. He must have realized that it wouldn't take the police long to track down any email Rachel had sent once their experts got to work on Jenny's computer. And if they found one that mentioned Coach Jack, they'd have a team at his doorstep any minute.

It seemed to fit. The business communication Jack told me he was expecting must have been pure fiction—an excuse to hurry off to his bedroom to check Ben's email. Jack surely knew how to do that; computers were his business. Ben might even have given Jack his email address back when they were setting times for coaching sessions. Yes, Jack must have found something that caused him to darken the house and try to rush me out the door. Maybe an email from Rachel warning Ben that I'd been asking questions about him.

Could Ben have received Rachel's email? I didn't see how—not if Jack had him locked up in this room. Yet Ben must have escaped somehow. And there must have been some kind of communication between him and Rachel. Otherwise how could his girlfriend have known where to meet him?

I leaned against the door to rest my arms and shoulders. And my brain. My thoughts were running in circles. If Ben had escaped, why did Jack run from the police? If Jack hadn't hurt him, why not just admit to the officers that he had let the runaway stay here for a bit? Tell them he was trying to get Ben to turn himself in, but he got away before Jack could pull it off.

As I considered the story Jack could have concocted, I found myself wondering if it could possibly be true. If Ben accidentally killed his brother, could he have turned to Jack for a place to hide? Could Jack simply have been trying to help him?

I shook my head. Why would Jack harbor a fugitive whose face was on the front page of every newspaper? Why did he lie to me about going to his aunt's funeral? Why did he run when the police pounded on his door? I couldn't think of any innocent reason why he would do those things.

Then did Jack kill Jessie?

I sank down on the bed and let my forehead drop into in my hands. My head was pounding, and I couldn't stop the thoughts that pulsed through it. Jack knew where the boys lived, so he could have been watching the house, waiting for an opportunity. He could have seen Tiffany drop Ben off early Thursday afternoon because he had a headache, but he wouldn't have known Jessie cut school that same morning. Did Little Brother show up unexpectedly and surprise Jack in some unspeakable act with Ben?

Suddenly I couldn't stop shaking. Gradually, I became aware that a draft of cold air was coming from somewhere over my head. The A/C had come on. The A/C? That meant the electricity was working! What was the matter with me? I hadn't even tried to turn on a light. I guess I'd just assumed Jack had turned off the electricity when the house went dark. Truth was, I'd given in to panic. Jumping up, I felt frantically around the edge of the doorway for a light switch. Found it. Then miracle of miracles, a track light on the ceiling responded to the flick of my finger.

Could the glow be visible from outside around the plywood? It was worth a try. I flicked the switch on and off five times. Paused. Five more times. Another pause. Five more. Leaving the light on, I climbed back up onto the file cabinets and began pounding and hollering again. Suddenly I stopped. I thought I'd heard something. Yes! A shout! A man's voice!

"Punta Gorda Police! Where are you?"

Chapter Seventeen

The two uniformed policemen who slid open the bedroom door a few minutes later were the most beautiful sight I'd seen in hours. I did what any normal hostage would do upon release. I burst into tears. "I'm so glad to see you," I blubbered.

"Easy, Ma'am," the heftier one said. "You're OK now. I'm Officer Shield, Punta Gorda Police, and this here's Officer Bevan. What's your name?"

"Anna Sebastian," I said, trying to steady my voice. "You sure got in fast. Thank God!"

"House wasn't locked. And this door was just jammed with two rubber doorstops." Shield looked me over. "You live here?"

"No. I was having dinner with Jack Braxton."

Bevan stepped forward. "He's gone?"

I nodded. "He locked me in here and slipped out the back door—at least that's what he said he was going to do."

"How long ago?" Bevan barked.

"I don't know. Maybe two hours. It was right after you came the first time—I guess it was you. When he heard the doorbell, he grabbed me and clamped his hand over my mouth." I felt more tears coming, fought them hard. "He held me like that till you left. Then he shoved me in this room and jammed the door." In the distance, I heard sirens.

"Bastard," Bevan muttered. "You his girlfriend?"

"No!" I glanced toward Shield, who seemed friendlier, but he remained silent. "I'm . . . well, we've had a few dates, but I'm certainly not his girlfriend."

"Any idea where he went?"

I was trembling from head to toe now, and my teeth chattered as the words tumbled out. "He parked in an empty lot a block up the street," I said, pointing. "He drives a Hyundai Santa Fe. Blue. He's probably long gone, but you've got to find him. He's been hiding Ben Tolliver."

A look passed between them before their eyes zeroed in on mine. Suddenly finding his voice, Shield asked, "What do you know about the missing boy?"

"I know he's been here."

"You saw him?"

"No. He's not here now. I'm pretty sure of that—unless he's tied up or . . . something." I shuddered involuntarily. "But I found a poem he wrote." I gestured toward the rollaway. "It was under this mattress."

"A poem?" The look they exchanged said they wondered if I'd gone mental.

"It's a long story," I said. A siren that seemed to be right outside the boarded window wailed, then dwindled to a stop. Footsteps pounded, coming closer. "I'm a Guardian ad Litem for Ben—a child advocate appointed by the court. He liked to write poetry, and . . . ." I broke off when four officers approached from the hallway. Bevan issued crisp instructions and joined one of them as they fanned out in different directions.

Shield stayed with me. Like a mom trying to calm a hysterical child, he said, "You look a little wobbly. Why don't we find a place to sit down?" He led me into the living room, where I sank onto the only soft chair. "Would you like a cup of coffee or something?" he asked.

"No, I'm all right," I lied.

He lowered his large frame onto the tweed couch across a corner from me and assumed a posture of practiced relaxation. Giving me what passed for a disarming smile, he said, "Let's start at the beginning."

I was still trying to decide exactly where the beginning was when Bevan returned. "Dirty dishes on the dining room table," he told Shield. "No sign of Braxton or the kid." Turning to me, he said,

"Ma'am, you said you found a poem and you think the Tolliver boy wrote it. May I see it?"

"It's, um, in my bra."

The tight line of his mouth twitched slightly at the corners. "We'll close our eyes."

Feeling supremely foolish, I turned my back and fished out the sweaty poem. "OK," I said. Bevan crossed over to me and held out his hand. With as much dignity as I could manage, I smoothed it out and gave it to him. He frowned at it. "Don't make much sense," he muttered.

"Ben's poetry can be pretty obscure," I said, stating the obvious.

"How about showing us where you found it," Shield said.

The two men engaged in muted conversation as I led them back to the guest room. "What made you look under the mattress?" Bevan asked.

"It happened by accident. I tripped over the foot of the bed, and toppled down onto the mattress. It slid halfway off the frame before I could stop it. And when I went to put it back, I spotted the sheet of paper lying on the springs."

I expected them to ask what I was doing in the guest room, but instead Bevan said, "Two of the detectives working the Tolliver case just called. They're on their way to the station. They want to talk to you if you're willing to go down there."

He was very polite, and I wondered what he'd have said if I refused. I didn't, of course. I was more than ready to talk to anyone who might be able to find Ben and Rachel—if they were still alive.

And to catch Jack Braxton.

Chapter Eighteen

Seated across the table from me in the police station's interview room, Detective Rex Underwood studied me the way a cat inspects a mouse. Not that he was disrespectful or surly; he was impeccably polite. But he sat like a panther ready to spring. Acne had left marks on his narrow face, and his hair, what there was of it, was dirty blonde. I guessed his age as early forties. "I hear you had an exciting night," he said with a smile that didn't reach his eyes. "Tell me what happened."

I poured out the whole story. My appointment as Guardian ad Litem on the Tolliver case. My relationship with both boys. Coach Jack and how he'd taken a special interest in Ben—and then in me.

"You were lovers?"

"No! We just had dinner a couple times. He broke one date because his aunt died and he had to fly to Nebraska—or so he told me. That just happened to be the same day Jessie was murdered." I heard the sarcasm in my voice. Answering his raised eyebrow, I said, "I did think it was a pretty big coincidence, but then yesterday he called, said he just got back in town, and invited me over for dinner. He sounded so normal, my suspicions . . . well, just sort of evaporated." I gave an embarrassed shrug. "So I went."

Shedding the panther posture, he leaned back, putting his hands behind his head. "And how did you end up locked up in a bedroom?"

I launched into the whole grim story. How Jack had suddenly turned into a different person after I mentioned my hunch that Rachel was emailing Ben from her friend Jenny's house. How he'd dashed unceremoniously from the table. How I'd followed him down the hall a bit later and found him hunched over his computer.

And how I'd stumbled—literally—onto Ben's poem under the mattress in the guest room.

"Braxton was still at his computer in the master bedroom?" Underwood asked.

"Yes."

"What were you doing in the guest room?"

"Well, I . . . ." I shuffled in my chair, feeling like a spy who's been caught red handed. Why had I been snooping around his house anyway? I did my best to explain. "After Jack started acting so strange, I just felt creepy. All the terrible suspicions I'd had earlier came roaring back—like the huge coincidence that he 'left town' the same day Jessie was murdered. Like his interest in Ben that seemed a bit . . . well . . . over the top."

My stomach knotted as I remembered how I'd felt as I stood outside Jack's bedroom trying to make sense out of his actions. "He'd seen me standing in the doorway," I told Underwood, "and I said I'd come down to use the bathroom. He promised he'd only be a few minutes, but I sensed it would be more than a few. The guest room was right across the hall, and I just glanced at it as I turned to start back up the hall. But a very nice computer station caught my eye, and I wondered why Jack wasn't using it. And something about the room struck me as strange. It seemed unnaturally clean—like someone had moved out of it and someone else had cleaned up behind him. I only meant to step far enough inside to look at the room's only picture but then, like I told you, I tripped and fell over the foot of the rollaway bed and found Ben's poem."

Underwood studied me long enough to make me uncomfortable. I couldn't tell if he believed anything I'd said or if he thought I was a nut case. Or worse.

"What did you do then?" he asked.

"I panicked! I dove for the bathroom and stuffed Ben's poem into my bra. All I could think about was getting out of there without letting Jack know that I knew Ben had been there. I was so scared."

"With good reason."

I continued my narrative, telling the detective how Jack had overpowered me when the police rang the doorbell and then trapped me in the guest room. After I finished my story, he made me go over every detail a dozen times—or so it seemed. Over and over, he asked the same questions. And I gave the same answers.

At last he said, "OK." He let his head drop back and rubbed his back for a moment. Massaging his right shoulder, he asked, "Anything else you want to add?"

I thought a moment. "Just a question."

"Shoot."

"I'm so amazed and so grateful— " My voice caught. "I'm so grateful the police showed up when they did. At first it seemed like a miracle—or mental telepathy or something—but then I remembered that Candy Owen promised to call you about Jenny's computer. Is that how you figured out Ben might be at Jack's?"

Underwood frowned at me, seeming to debate whether to honor me with an answer. Finally he said, "Yeah. After Rachel York's foster mom called us, my partner sent a team over to the friend's house. It didn't take them long to find the kids' Hotmail account. The girl's email said you'd been asking questions about Coach Jack and if Ben was hiding there, he wouldn't be safe for long. We already had the coach's name on our list of people to interview, so we knew where he lived." He paused to let that sink in.

"'If Ben was hiding there,'" I repeated. "That sounds like Rachel wasn't sure Ben was there."

Pursing his lips, he said, "Could be she just took an educated guess after talking to you. Anyway, the email begged Ben to turn himself in before you went to the police."

"Did you find an answer from Ben?"

Underwood shook his head. "The only one from Ben was sent the day after his brother's murder, and all it said was, 'Don't send any more email. I'll contact you when I can.'"

I let out my breath as if I'd been holding it, which I probably had been. "Rachel's email didn't say anything about meeting Ben?"

"Nope." Underwood studied his fingernails.

"It doesn't make sense," I murmured.

"Unless he thought someone was monitoring his email," Underwood said.

Of course! Ben must have realized Jack knew how to get into the Hotmail account. Why else would he have told Rachel not to send any more? "But if they were planning to meet, they must have found some way to contact each other."

"Seems that way, but we haven't found it yet."

"Do you think Ben is still alive?" I asked.

"Hope so."

"If he didn't show up where Rachel expected to meet him, surely she would have gone back home. And I gather she hasn't?"

"No." He picked at something under one of his fingernails. "In fact, she bought two bus tickets to Ft. Myers this morning." Glancing at his watch, he corrected himself. "Guess that's yesterday now. Anyway, the clerk at the Greyhound station recognized her picture, and he recalled that someone was with her. A guy. The clerk didn't get a good look at him but said he was wearing a ball cap. Unfortunately, the bus left at 10:10 a.m., and the girl wasn't reported missing till noon. We haven't picked up their trail yet, but we will. Did Ben ever mention anyone he knew in Ft. Myers—relatives, friends?"

I thought hard. "He was living in Fort Myers when he first entered the DCF system, and his paternal grandmother may live near there, but I don't think he'd go to her."

"We've already checked her out. Anyone else?"

"Not that I can think of."

"Well, it was a long shot, but sometimes Guardians hear things case workers don't." Underwood shifted sideways in his chair, stretched his long legs, and looked at me with a raised eyebrow. "The poem you found—did you read it?"

"No, I didn't have time. All I was saw was the title and Ben's name."

"I can't make head or tail of it."

"Ben's poems are like that. Could I see it? Since I know him and I've read his other poems, I might spot something you wouldn't."

Without a word, Underwood pulled the wrinkled sheet from a folder and passed it over to me. I read it and shivered. It was as obscure as his first poem and even darker.

"Well?" Underwood asked after a minute. "Can you make sense of it?"

I shook my head. "He used some of the same images in an earlier poem, but I don't know what they represent. Could I have a copy of this? Something might come to me later."

He considered that for a second, then left the room. In a few minutes he returned and handed me a clean copy. "You said Ben gave you other poems?"

"Two of them. I'll bring them to you tomorrow. After his English teacher told me he had a real gift for poetry, I always encouraged him to write. I used to call him Edgar Allen Tolliver to tease him, and that always made him blush."

Underwood let out a short "Hmmp" and mumbled, "Figures."

"What figures?" I asked.

He shook his head absently, frowning at the bedraggled original of Ben's poem, which he still held in his hand. "You know this kid. How mentally disturbed is he?"

Surprised, I asked, "You still suspect him of killing his brother?"

Underwood shrugged. "I suspect everybody. It's my job."

His comment triggered a memory. "Ben's mother told me she thought you suspected her and her husband."

He shook his head. "Not anymore. Both of them were at work during the whole period the murder could have happened. That's confirmed by staff."

"But you still suspect Ben even though Jack abducted him?"

He worked at his fingernails again. "We don't have evidence of abduction. Suspicions, sure. But for all we know, the kid came to Braxton looking for a place to hide."

"But why would Jack let him stay? He knew Ben was wanted by the police. If he really wanted to help him, he would have called someone—if not the police, then DCF, or a lawyer, or me." I felt my blood pressure rising. "And if Jack was innocent, why did he run from the police?"

"I didn't say he was innocent, just that the kid could have come to his house of his own free will." He gave me an ugly smile. "A bit of candy dropped on his doorstep, you know?"

Chapter Nineteen

It was after midnight when I finally tumbled into bed, and my body ached from head to toe. Extra-strength Tylenol diminished the pain enough to let me drift into a restless sleep, but I woke long before sunup. I kept seeing Ben's wary blue eyes, the smattering of freckles on his cheeks, his winsome but rare smile. I couldn't get his face out of my mind.

Or his haunting poetry

When the clock struck five, I gave up on sleep and poured myself a cup of coffee. Thus fortified, I laid the copy of Ben's latest poem on the kitchen table. I hadn't read it very carefully last night with Underwood's eyes boring holes in my head. Now I took time with every word.

FORSAKEN ANGEL
by Ben Tolliver

Angel fell into fire and water;
forsaken angel, guilty of nothing,
punished forever.

Mad dogs swarm the city,
Bulldog bares his teeth
then and now.

Peace is a phantom; only death is real.
Three against two; two against three.
And one against all.

This time the forsaken angel was in the title. And it seemed to be a particular person—someone who fell into fire and water. That had to be Jessie, didn't it? Jessie fell—or was pushed—into the water. But where could fire fit in?

Giving up, I moved on. *Mad dogs swarm the city. Bulldog bares his teeth then and now.* The dogs that howled and broke down gates in Ben's first poem now swarmed the city. And one of them had a name. Bulldog.

Was Jack Bulldog? Last night Jack had transformed before my eyes from an unusually nice guy into someone I didn't know—or want to know. Someone vicious and dangerous. Like a bulldog! Ben had been at Jack's house, and he'd written this poem while he was there.

Still, if Jack was Bulldog, who were the other dogs—the ones Ben mentioned in two different poems? Back when Ben gave me his first poem, *The Dark,* I'd suspected that the howling dogs in it referred to the drug scene. Of course, I could have been wrong about that. But the case file was full of allegations of drug use. And Vera Mosely seemed convinced that the driver of a BMW she saw parked at the trailer was dealing.

Underwood told me he suspected everyone, but he hadn't mentioned the BMW driver. Was he on the detective's list of suspects? I decided to ask him when I dropped off Ben's poems at the police station before work this morning. I also wanted to stop at the Tolliver's trailer to give Tiffany and Gordy the copies of Ben's poems I'd made for them. I was very interested in their reaction.

Underwood was on his way out the door when he met me in the police department's waiting area. He took the poems with a quick nod, but didn't invite me back into his office cubicle "Any new insights?" he asked in the hurried tone of a guy already late for an important date.

"More questions than insight. There are some vicious dogs in Ben's poems, and Jack could certainly be one of them. But it also occurred to me that the dogs might relate to the drug scene. One of the Tolliver's neighbors, Vera Mosely, told me she saw a BMW parked at their trailer, and she thought he might be dealing."

Underwood cut me off. "Yeah, we talked with Ms. Mosely."

"Then the driver is on your list of suspects?"

"Yep." He took a half step backwards toward the door. "Anything else?"

"I . . . guess not."

"Well, call me if you think of something." With that, he was out the door.

The reception I got from Gordy Tolliver was warmer despite the fact that he answered my knock wearing sleeper shorts and an undershirt. "What brings you here at the crack of dawn," he said, greeting me with his usual friendly grin that exposed lower teeth thrusting beyond his upper jaw.

Still in her bathrobe, Tiffany appeared behind him at the trailer door. "Has something happened?" she asked tremulously.

My heart went out to her, and I felt guilty intruding into their privacy. "I wondered if you knew that Rachel York ran away from her foster home yesterday," I said, trying for an even tone. Was that only yesterday?

Gordy answered but didn't step out of the doorway. "Yeah, that Detective Underwood was over, said the girl left a note saying she was going to meet Ben to try to talk him into turning himself in."

"So that means Ben's OK, don't you think?" Tiffany asked me.

"I sure hope so," I said.

"You haven't heard anything more?"

"No, and I'm sorry to bother you so early but I wanted to show you something." I held up the slim three-ring notebook I had put together for them.

"What is it?" Tiffany asked, peering over her husband's shoulder.

"Ben's poetry."

If I'd been speaking Swahili, they couldn't have looked more bewildered.

"My son wrote poetry?" Same tone Gordy might use to say, "The cat threw up on the rug."

"Yes, and he's very talented. I thought you might like to read these." I stepped off the worn dirt path onto the grass. I wasn't going to hold this conversation with Gordy hanging out the open trailer door and Tiffany standing on tiptoe trying to peek over his shoulder.

Tiffany wriggled around her husband and scrambled down the steps. "Let me see." I opened the notebook to the first poem, holding it out for her to read. Gordy hastened down the steps and stared at the page as if he could read it upside down. "It's just a mumbo-jumbo," Tiffany said finally. But she took the notebook from me.

"I can't say I understand it," I said, "but I don't think it's mumbo jumbo. I think it's full of symbolism—words that stand for something else. In fact, I'm pretty sure some of the language he uses comes from Bible." Noting the blank looks on both their faces, I added, "Words he might have heard in Sunday School or from someone who taught him about God."

"Mama," Gordy said with a roll of his eyes.

Surprised, I asked him, "Your mother?"

Tiffany answered for him. "No, my mother. We lived with her for awhile when the children were little. The boys called her Mama. She was real religious." Flipping a page, she frowned at the poem titled, "First Down."

"This one's about football," she said.

"Lemme see," Gordy demanded. Stepping down beside his wife, he stared at the poem in stunned silence.

Tiffany flipped to the last poem and read the title aloud softly. "Forsaken Angel." Her eyes darted from left to right as she read.

"You gonna stand out here forever?" Gordy asked with uncharacteristic sharpness. Tiffany didn't seem to hear; her attention was fixed on Ben's poem. "Come on," Gordy said, taking the poetry notebook from his wife's hand. "I'm ready for breakfast."

A veil seemed to drop over Tiffany's eyes. "All right, I'm coming."

Gordy waited for her to climb the steps, then clomped up after her, the notebook in his hand. Turning back to me, he said, "Thanks, Anna. Appreciate it." The door closed behind him with a decisive thunk.

Chapter Twenty

After I left the Tollivers' trailer, I took a short detour on my way to work to stop by Kate's house. I wanted to fill her in on the mind-blowing events that had happened since I saw her Sunday evening. I found her in a flurry of preparation for a memorial service she would be conducting at eleven. Still she listened to my story with undivided attention and let out a gasp when I gave her the poem I had discovered under the mattress in Jack's guest room. Murmuring a hundred apologies because she hadn't found time to track down the biblical imagery in Ben's earlier poem, she promised to get to it right after the memorial service.

I got to work a few minutes late, and I felt like I was only half there. Somehow I got through my regular Tuesday morning cash-flow presentation for the doctors and staff, but all I really wanted to do was sleep. Or cry. For hours. Possibly days.

"Are you all right, Anna?" Dr. Johansen's question startled me as he fell into step with me on the way back to my small bookkeeping office.

"Oh, yes, fine," I lied. "Thanks, Dr. Jo."

"You didn't seem your usual chipper self at the meeting."

"I think I'm just tired. Thanks for asking."

"I know it's not easy, getting over to the nursing home every day to see your mom. If you need some time off or anything, just say so." He stopped walking and faced me. "You're doing a great job here, and we don't want to lose you."

I'd been holding together pretty well, but his kindness was exactly what I didn't need. Or maybe I did, but it shook my composure and I felt tears flood my eyes. "That helps a lot," I managed. I made it to the privacy of my cubicle before I lost it completely. Closing the door behind me, I let the tears stream down my face. It was too much. My ruined marriage. Alistair. Mom. Jessie. Ben. Jack. It was way too much.

When finally I collected myself, I checked my cell phone for messages and discovered I'd forgotten to turn it on this morning. It showed a voice mail from Tiffany Tolliver, left at 10:05 a.m. Her recorded voice was low. "Anna, I need to talk to you. Can you meet me at McDonald's after the lunch rush? Any time between two and four. Don't call me back; just come if you can." She was quiet so long I thought that was the end of the message. Then she added, "It's about Ben's poems."

By three o'clock Tuesday afternoon, the McDonald's in Promenades Mall was deserted except for an older couple chatting by the window and a group of men in sweat-soaked T-shirts savoring burgers and jokes at a corner table. I walked toward the order counter, but didn't see Tiffany.

"Help you?" asked the bored young woman behind the cash register.

"I'm looking for Tiffany Tolliver."

The woman scowled. "Not in today."

Not in? "She told me she was working today."

"Supposed to," she snorted. "She didn't show. Called in sick. Again."

Sick? "That's funny. She left me a message this morning asking me to meet her here." *To tell me something about Ben's poems.*

"Hey Mike," the woman hollered over her shoulder. "What's the story on Tiffany? This lady wants to know."

A minute or so later, a harried young man hustled past the French fry basket. "Tiffany didn't come in today," he told me.

"Do you know why not? She told me she'd be here."

Mike shrugged.

"You gonna order?" snapped the cashier.

"Oh. I'll just have a small coffee."

I downed half the cup on my way back to my car and threw the rest in the grass. It was too hot for coffee. I should have ordered iced tea, but my mind had been elsewhere. Why did Tiffany ask me to meet her here if she wasn't planning to come in? What changed her mind?

Frustrated and disgusted, I tried to call her. No answer. A vague sense of uneasiness edged out some of my frustration. She'd sounded funny on the voice mail, speaking so softly I could hardly hear her. She said she wanted to tell me something about Ben's poems. I rechecked my cell phone. She'd left the message at 10:05, but hadn't shown up for work at eleven. Odd.

Ten minutes later I pulled up in front of the Tolliver place. Tiffany's ancient black Plymouth sat in the driveway, but no one answered my knock on the trailer door. "Tiffany!" I shouted. "Tiffany! Are you home?" Silence.

I started back toward my Ford, then stopped. What if she was sick—really sick? What if she needed a doctor? Telling myself I was probably overreacting, I walked back up the dirt path to the trailer, mounted the metal steps and knocked again. Still no answer. I tried the handle. To my surprise, it yielded to my touch. I cracked open the heavy door and peeked inside. The stench assaulted my nostrils before I saw her.

On the living room couch, Tiffany slumped in a pool of vomit.

I let out a stifled scream. "Tiffany!" She didn't respond. Her only visible eye was wide open and staring. Sprinting across the room, I touched her back with my hand, hoping to feel the rise and fall of breathing. I didn't. Fighting hysteria, I pressed her neck. It was ice cold. There was no sign of a pulse. I stumbled out the door and threw up on the grass.

Shaking all over, I made it back to my car and leaned against it for support. I fumbled for my cell phone, and called 911.

In spite of the sun beating down on the parched day, I shivered as I waited for the police. The air was still as death. No sound of sirens yet. Feeling alone and scared, I glanced at the cell phone I still held in my hand. With shaking fingers, I pressed Kate's number. "I'm sorry to bother you," I told her after the church secretary connected us, "but I needed to hear a friendly voice."

"Are you OK?"

"No." In a rush, I told her what happened.

"My God!" she exploded. "You found the body? And you're still there? By yourself? Do you want me to come?"

"No, the dispatcher promised the police would be here right away. I just needed to hear a word of sanity. My world has gone mad. I can't stop thinking about Tiffany and . . . oh, Kate, it was so awful!" I told her about my visit with the Tollivers this morning and the message Tiffany left on my phone a short time later. "She was whispering, and she said she wanted to tell me something about Ben's poems. I keep wondering if whatever she wanted me to know could have anything to do with her death. I don't see how it could, but the timing sure is spooky. I guess you haven't had a chance to study the poems yet."

"No, but the Memorial Service is over, and I've almost finished up here. As soon as I get back to my house, I'll start on that project, and I'll call you if I turn up anything."

As I closed my phone, a female voice startled me. "You all right, Dearie?" Vera Mosely bustled around my car and patted my shoulder. "Looks like you're not feeling too good."

As I stared into the solicitous face of the Tollivers' across-the-street neighbor, I pointed to the trailer and choked out a few words. "It's not me; it's her. She's dead!" In the distance, a siren whined.

"Dead!" Vera's eyes widened. "How?"

"I don't know. She threw up. Slumped over. That's how I found her."

Vera gave a knowing nod. "OD'd, I bet."

Taken aback by her obvious lack of sympathy, I asked, "You still think she was doing drugs?"

She raised an eyebrow. "Yeah, and she had a visitor this morning. A man." Giving her wide hips a suggestive little twist, she added, "After her husband left for work." Emphasis on *husband*. "Guy drove by real slow, then parked down the street and walked back. Stood there a bit looking at the trailer before he walked up."

"Did he go inside?"

"I don't know. He knocked, and she opened the door and they stood there ten or fifteen minutes talking. But then my soap started, so I didn't see if he went in."

"Did you recognize him? The man?"

"Uh-uh. Or the car either. He was driving something silver. Smaller. I got its license number."

"What time was that?"

She frowned. "Well, my soap started at 10:30. It was a bit before that."

After Tiffany called me. About the time she should have been leaving for work. "What did the man look like?"

"Not real tall—under six feet, I'd say. Kind of slender but nicely built. He had short curly hair."

Suddenly I felt so dizzy I had to reach for the car to steady myself. "What color was it—his hair?"

"Reddish blonde, I'd say. Why, you know him?"

Trying to quell the bile that crept into my throat, I shook my head vigorously. "I hope not." But I had an ugly feeling I did.

Chapter Twenty-one

By the time I got home it was after five, and all I wanted was a long soak in the tub—something to wash away the horror of the day. But the light on my answering machine was blinking, and I couldn't seem to walk past it without pushing *play.*

The voice was Kate's. "Anna, call me. I've been working on Ben's poems, and I've turned up something interesting."

A minute later I had her on the phone. After I relayed more details of my afternoon's horror story, she asked, "Have the police figured out how Tiffany died?"

"I don't know. Underwood showed up at the scene and asked me a lot of questions about her history of drug use, but he didn't give out any information. The neighbor across the street told the police she saw a guy at the Tollivers' trailer this morning." I took a deep breath. "He had curly, reddish hair. Like Jack."

She let out a low whistle, and for a moment I forgot that I'd called in response to her voice mail. Suddenly remembering, I said, "Your phone message said you found out something about Ben's poems?"

There was a long silence. Then she asked, "Did Jessie have epilepsy?"

"What?"

"Here's an idea" she said. "Why don't you come over? It's kind of complicated to explain over the phone, and I have chicken casserole in my fridge. You sound like you could use a change of scene. After you've taken in some nourishment, we can look at Ben's poems together and I'll explain why I asked."

Gratitude brought a sudden lump to my throat. "That sounds wonderful." In truth, I didn't think I could face a whole evening in my mother's empty house, playing and replaying the memories of the last few hours.

Foregoing the long soak, I settled for a quick shower and clean jeans. Half an hour later, I sat at Kate's kitchen table, watching her serve me a hot scoop of something that contained chicken, broccoli, cheese and other unknown substances. "Potluck dinner leftovers," she said.

"Don't you ever, um, cook?"

She laughed, lifting my spirits. "Only when there's a gap in the congregational supply line. I pretty much exist on meatloaf, chicken casseroles, and Jell-O salad."

I didn't feel hungry—an appetite seemed almost indecent after the tragedy of the day. But Kate decreed we would eat before we worked, and after the first bite I discovered I was ravenous. I hadn't eaten much breakfast, and I'd left my lunch on the Tollivers' front lawn. Gradually, the warmth of the food and her cheerful chatter began to erode the bone-chill I had brought with me. We topped off the meal with a Klondike bar before I said, "I can't stand it a minute longer. Why did you ask if Jessie had epilepsy?"

"I'll show you," Kate said. "Let's move to the dining room."

A stack of books occupied one end of her oak table. Kate sat down beside them and motioned me into the chair next to her. Spreading out Ben's three poems, she said, "Once I finally got to these, I spent over an hour on them. I'll skip my wild goose chases and give you the short version. Otherwise we'd be here all night, and I have a meeting at eight. I thought the poem Ben wrote after his brother's death—the one you found at Jack's house—was the most likely to contain something significant, so I began with that one." She picked up *Forsaken Angel* and read the first stanza aloud.

Angel fell into fire and water;
forsaken angel, guilty of nothing,
punished forever.

Kate pulled a thick book from the stack. "Young's *Analytical Concordance to the Bible*," she announced. "My favorite concordance."

"What's a concordance?"

"It's a bit like a dictionary. It lists all the key words in the Bible, but instead of giving definitions, it shows the chapter and verse for every place each word appears. By the way"—she pointed to an equally heavy book at the other end of the table—"I brought another copy over from the church library. If you want, you can take it home in case you decide to work on the poems yourself." Turning back to Young, she said, "OK, let's find the first word in Ben's poem, *angel*." As Kate located the page, I slid close enough to read it with her.

The word *angel* occupied almost three columns. "I looked up several of these references in the Bible," Kate said, "but none of them seemed to fit Ben's poem, so I moved on to *fire*. I was hoping to discover a verse that combined the words, *angel, fire,* and *water*. I found a few that contained *fire* and *water*. And eureka! One of them was about someone *falling* into fire and water." Kate pointed out the reference she had underlined: *Matthew 17:15.*

Reaching for a Revised Standard Version of the Bible, she flipped to the book of Matthew and located chapter seventeen. "This is a story about a man who knelt before Jesus and begged him to heal his son." She began to read at verse fifteen.

Lord, have mercy on my son, for he is an epileptic and he suffers terribly; for he often falls into the fire, and often into the water."

Kate looked up at me. "It doesn't say anything about an angel, but the thought occurred to me that 'angel' could simply be a term of endearment for a child, the way a parent might address a son or daughter as 'angel' or 'my angel.'"

"So Ben's first line could mean 'a child fell into fire and water.'" A child. Like Jessie. "And the boy in the Bible story fell into fire and water because he was having a seizure."

"Exactly. If Ben's mother read this story to him when he was young, it could easily have stuck in his mind, especially if he had an epileptic brother."

"It wasn't his mother who read him the Bible; it was his grandmother—Tiffany's mother. I learned that this morning when I stopped by to show the Tollivers Ben's poems."

We were both quiet for a few minutes, each thinking our own grim thoughts. "If Jessie had epilepsy," I said finally, "I think Candy Owen would have told me." Still, epilepsy was common among children with Fetal Alcohol Syndrome, so maybe Jessie was taking medication that controlled it, and no one bothered to mention it. Sensing Kate's gaze on me, I voiced these speculations. "But even if Jessie did have seizures, I don't see how that could have anything to do with his death. The police seem pretty sure he didn't just fall into the pond—he was killed by a blow to his head."

"Yeah," Kate said, blowing out a long puff of air. "Well, let's move on. I think I know where Ben's dogs came from." She read aloud.

> Mad dogs swarm the city,
> Bulldog bares his teeth
> then and now.

Glancing at a pad of penciled notes, Kate said, "There weren't as many references to 'dogs' as there were to 'angels'. I found five that included both 'dogs' and 'city', but nothing fell into place. Then I looked back at *The Dark*, Ben's first poem, and reread this line: *The dogs howl, break down the gates.* When I looked up *gates*, I discovered that one of the 'gate' references followed a verse I'd already found under 'dogs' and 'city.' It's in Revelation 22, verses 14 and 15." She slid the Bible between us, flipped to its last book, and read aloud from the twenty-second chapter.

Blessed are those who wash their robes, that they may have the right to the tree of life and that they may enter the city by the gates. Outside are the dogs and sorcerers and fornicators and murderers and idolaters, and everyone who loves and practices falsehood.

As I gazed at Kate in bewilderment, she interpreted the passage for me. "I can picture Ben's grandmother teaching Ben that 'city' meant 'heaven' and that 'people who washed their robes' meant 'people who kept themselves pure from sin.' She probably told her grandson that if he wasn't good, he wouldn't get into heaven because bad people get locked out of heaven's gates. I hate it when parents use religion to try to scare their kids into being good, but some do it."

What an impact Mama must have had on her impressionable young grandson! "So the 'dogs' represent bad people—people who won't go to heaven?"

"I think so."

"But in Ben's poems the bad people aren't locked out; they break down the gates and swarm the city."

"Of course. Ben always turns the Bible's message upside down."

I read the strange line one more time. *Mad dogs swarm the city, Bulldog bares his teeth then and now.* "Bulldog," I said aloud, glancing up at Kate.

"There's no bulldog in the Bible," she said quietly. "Do you think it could be a nickname?"

A nickname! I felt a sudden rush of adrenalin. A nickname Tiffany recognized? I thought about my visit with the Tollivers this morning. Tiffany had been so focused on Ben's poem, she hadn't even heard her husband nagging her to go inside. And when he finally took the poetry notebook from her, her eyes seemed to go dead.

"I have a feeling something in Ben's last poem jumped out at Tiffany this morning, Kate. I saw it in her face. I don't think she would have caught the 'holy city' stuff. But she could have noticed a familiar nickname. I wonder if she wanted to tell me something about Bulldog!"

Bulldog. The worst of the scumballs who should have been locked out of the city's gates, but weren't. Someone Tiffany knew. A drug dealer? Maybe someone who drove a black BMW? "What kind of person might pick up the tag 'bulldog'?" I wondered aloud.

"Georgia Bulldogs," Kate said with a sudden smile.

"What?"

"University of Georgia." She chuckled. "Obviously you're not a sports fan." Catching my look, she added, "I wasn't serious. What's the matter?"

"Jack Braxton went to the University of Georgia."

Chapter Twenty-two

As I left Kate's house, my mind wasn't on the road; I was thinking about Jack. Jack was a Georgia Bulldog. Did Ben and his teammates use this nickname? Had Ben talked about Bulldog the Coach at home? Did Tiffany make the connection when she spotted the name in Ben's poem? Is that what she wanted to tell me?

If Tiffany recognized Jack as the Bulldog in Ben's poem, maybe she called him—asked him to come over, then confronted him. I was pretty sure Jack had given Ben his phone number, so his mother probably knew how to contact him. It wouldn't have been a very smart thing to do, but Tiffany wasn't the most rational person I knew. And Jack had been at the Tollivers' trailer on the morning Tiffany died—I was almost certain of that.

A myriad of speculations swam in my head. Where were Ben and Rachel? Underwood said Rachel bought two bus tickets to Fort Myers, but the trail vanished from there. The ticket agent remembered Rachel, but didn't get a good look at the guy who was with her. Did the runaways actually board the bus? Since the depot was in Port Charlotte, the two teens would have needed to cross the Peace River Bridge to get there. How could they do that without someone spotting them? Rachel might have talked a friend into driving her, especially a male friend. She was beautiful and outgoing, and boys were attracted to her. Or she could have hitch-hiked. At the time she bought the tickets, she hadn't yet been reported missing, so an unsuspecting stranger could have offered her a ride. But Ben? How could he risk hitch-hiking when his face was all over the media? And he didn't have many friends—certainly not the kind who would help out a buddy who was wanted by the police. The more I thought about it, the more trouble I had believing that Ben had been with Rachel at the bus station yesterday morning.

Maybe Rachel went there with someone else. But no, her note said she was going to meet Ben. Could the bus clerk have been wrong when he identified Rachel's picture as the girl who bought two tickets to Fort Myers? He hadn't been able to describe the boy—or man—who was with her. How reliable was his memory?

What if Rachel and Ben didn't take the bus to Fort Myers? What if they never left town? What if they were hiding somewhere right under our noses?

Where could they go? The police were checking all their family and friends. The whole county had seen their pictures in the papers and on TV. They would need to find food and water. How could they possibly do that without someone recognizing them?

The one thing I knew for sure was that Ben had been at Jack's house in Punta Gorda. I thought about Jack's neighborhood. A lot of the homes stood empty now. Their owners had boarded up the broken windows, tarped the roof, and now waited out the repairs in the comfort of another home "up north,"—or for the less fortunate, in a FEMA trailer. For all I knew, Ben and Rachel could be holed up in one of those deserted houses. Lots of people left food on their shelves. Bottled water too—for hurricane preparedness.

I sat at the Route 41 intersection arguing with myself. The sun was sinking rapidly, but I probably still had an hour of daylight. *Don't play detective,* I told myself. *Turn right. Go home. Check on Mom.* But what if Ben and Rachel really were camped in one of the hurricane-damaged houses while the police spent their energy looking for them in Fort Myers? I turned left toward Punta Gorda.

By the time I crossed the bridge over the Peace River, I had a plan. If my hunch was correct that Ben had taken refuge in an abandoned house, it stood to reason he hadn't strayed very far from Jack's place on Grace Street. He surely wouldn't cross Route 41—too much traffic, activity, people, lights. He probably wouldn't cross the well-traveled Olympia either. Or Shreve Road. Too much open space to cover. No, he'd stay somewhere in the triangle bounded by

Route 41 on the east and the two diagonals to the west, Shreve on the south and Olympia on the north.

The hurricane had hit this little section so hard it was virtually deserted save for a few stalwarts and the ever-present construction workers. In one of these blown-out homes, a pair of runaway teens could secure a roof over their heads and probably enough of the essentials of life to tide them over for awhile. If Ben and Rachel weren't in Ft. Myers, they were somewhere in this triangle. I would bet on it.

By the time I reached Henry Street, the sun was close to the treetops. I turned onto McGregor and began a systematic cris-cross of the streets. The neighborhood looked like a war zone. Mountains of rubble lined the curbs. Roofs had been ripped apart, windows shattered, carports reduced to kindling. Nearly a third of the homes displayed the painted *R.O.E.* across the front, giving Right of Entry to insurance agents and demolition workers to buildings that were slated for destruction.

As I drove, I tried to project myself into Ben's brain. If I were a fifteen-year-old runaway, where would I hide? Not in a house with gaping holes or blown-out doors and windows that no one had bothered to board up. No, that kind of place would be too vulnerable. Anyone could just walk in. A home whose windows were covered with boards or aluminum shutters would have the advantage that a flashlight or candle wouldn't show up at night. On the other hand, gaining access to these structures without attracting attention would be virtually impossible.

On William Street, I paused in front of a yellow concrete-block house. In spite of a hole in the roof that exposed the rafters over what appeared to be the living room, part of the house looked inhabitable. I searched for a possible means of access—a single broken window or a storm shutter missing. I didn't see one, but that didn't mean it wasn't there. I grabbed a small notebook and a pencil from my glove compartment and jotted down the address before I crept on up the street.

At Route 41, I cut through the parking lot of the closed-down bank and came back west on McKenzie. Midway down the block, I paused in front of a pink frame. Some of its windows were boarded, and the roof had been tarped with blue plastic. I focused on a small boarded window on the side of the house, low enough to climb into. Could Ben have taken off the plywood, crawled in, unlocked a door—and perhaps found a key to a back or side door somewhere in the house—then replaced the plywood? I doubted it. In the daylight, someone might see him. At night, the pounding would make too much noise. Still, it was a possibility. I recorded the address in my notebook.

Turning left on Berry Street, I paused in front of a sand-colored stucco. Plywood covered the front windows, and the side windows were either boarded or intact. I passed the house, then looked back to inspect the other side. A small, high window, perhaps a bathroom, was broken out but not boarded. It was too high to crawl into from the ground, but Ben could have stood on something—maybe an upside-down garbage can he pilfered somewhere in the neighborhood. I noted the address. My plan was simply to explain my theory to Detective Underwood and give him the addresses I was recording.

Turning east on Linda Street, I spotted a crew of workmen on the roof of a tan house on my right, and I heard the shouts and bangs of their back-breaking task. Across the street, a dirty white block home caught my attention. As I approached, I noticed that the windows on the west side of the house were protected by opaque fiberglass shutters, a horizontal style commonly used with jalousie windows in older homes. Slowly, I drove by the house. In the front, a small window, perhaps for a kitchen, was covered by the same kind of shutter. A large living-room-type window had been boarded shut. After I crept by, I braked and looked back over my shoulder to study the east side of the house. Something struck me as odd about a long, narrow window toward the back, but I couldn't put my finger on it.

I continued up the street, turned around in a driveway, came back, and paused in a spot where I could get a clearer view of the east side of the house. Darkness was coming fast now and I was looking into the sunset. I had to shield my eyes with my hand in order to see the window that had puzzled me. I gazed at it for a long time. It was another jalousie window, protected by the same kind of opaque shutters I'd seen on the front of the house. Nothing strange about that. So what bothered me about it?

Finally I saw it. In the upper three-quarters of the window, the shutters totally covered the window frame. But around the lower section, a black frame was visible. How could that be? Suddenly I saw why. The lower horizontal shutter was on the inside of the house! Although the window was narrow, it was plenty wide enough for two slim teens to crawl through. Could they have removed the shutter, broken out the window pane to gain entry, and then somehow propped the shutter on the inside to cover the hole?

Chapter Twenty-three

Go home! my inner voice commanded. *Call the police—talk to Underwood.* But what could I tell him? That I'd located a house on Linda Street that seemed a remote possibility for the teenagers' hideout? That some fiberglass shutters might have been moved from the outside to the inside of a window—and it could mean something? Or nothing. And I'd have to admit I'd been playing detective.

Across the street and two houses to the west, one of the workmen climbed down from the roof and pulled out a jug of water from the back of his truck. I watched him for a moment, wondering if he'd ever seen the runaway teens and arguing with myself about whether to ask him. My better judgment lost the debate, and I pulled to the curb in front of an abandoned and overgrown blue house, just east of the suspicious white one. As I ambled down the street toward the construction site, a sweating workman stopped drinking from his water jug and frowned at me. "Hello," I said cheerily. "May I ask you a question?"

The man was dark-skinned, probably Latin. He smiled, shaking his head. "No English." He held up a finger, signaling for me to wait, and shouted a string of Spanish to one of the men on the roof. A moment later, the man clambered down the ladder. "You have question?" he asked as he approached me.

"Yes. That white house over there," I said, pointing. "Have you ever seen a teenage boy or girl around there?"

"Boy? Girl? No. That house, it is empty. No one live there. The hurricane—"

I cut him off. "After the storm, maybe someone broke in?"

"Break in? No." He smiled. "No police." He spread his hands as if that explained everything.

I thanked the workman, who stared after me scratching his head. Had I really thought Ben or Rachel would enter or leave the house when workers were around? *Stupid, Anna, stupid.*

As I started back across the street, I glanced left and noticed an older couple emerging from the faded pink house opposite the construction site, two doors west of the white house. The man, rail thin, appeared about a hundred. The woman who dragged him by the arm probably ate enough for both of them. They stopped in the middle of the street and looked both ways, shading their eyes with their hands as if searching for something. I strolled over and greeted them brightly. "Lovely evening, isn't it?"

"Would be if the roof tiles they promised ever get here," the man grumbled.

All three of us turned to gaze at the couple's roof. Unlike most of the houses in the neighborhood, theirs displayed no blue tarp. It had been "dried in" by a process called hot mopping, which made a water-tight seal before the colorful and popular concrete roof tiles were laid.

I glanced toward the workers across the street, who were now silhouetted against the spreading orange of the sky. "You're getting a new roof already?" I asked. "Aren't you lucky!"

"Will be if they ever get here," the man grunted.

"Before Charley hit, we had a contract with Dr. Goodroof to replace our shingles with concrete tile," the woman explained. "They were supposed to start in August, the day before the storm, but they called it off because of the forecast. So you're right; we really did get lucky. We're the Halls, by the way. Olive and Dick."

"Anna Sebastian." I sustained the chit-chat a few more minutes, giving them my best smile while I wondered how to inquire about Ben without making a ton of explanations. "Have you had much trouble with vandalism in this neighborhood?" I asked.

"Not really," said Olive Hall.

I pressed on, trying for a casual, small-talky tone. "I've heard teens have been breaking into some of these boarded up homes. You haven't noticed any problems like that on your street?" The wide sweep of my arm took in half a block, but it centered on the white house.

Olive shook her head, but her husband tilted his chin upwards. "Unless that street lamp was vandalism," he growled. I followed his pointing finger and spotted the tall, dark outline of a streetlight directly across from the white house. "Somebody—or some thing—broke it out over yonder."

"When did that happen?" I asked.

He squinted with the effort of thinking. "Can't quite remember. It's been awhile. It could have been kids, I suppose. Or loose tiles blowing around."

Was it storm damage? Or had a teenage fugitive pitched a rock in the wee hours, preferring darkness?

The sun had dropped below the horizon, and the workers were packing up to leave. I wished the Halls good luck with their new roof and walked back up the street to my Focus. I stood beside the car for a few minutes, watching the Halls disappear inside their home, apparently giving up on the promised delivery of roof tiles. The workers across the street piled into their pickup and roared off. After the day's construction racket, the stillness of the evening felt eerie. Forlorn. I got back into my car.

Through my windshield, I had a clear view of the east side of the white house. The untended bushes in the yard I had parked in front of stretched across the lot line to within a few feet of the window next door—the window I was so curious about. If I had enough nerve, I could make my way along the edge of that dense growth. Without even leaving the cover of its branches, I might get a pretty good look through the suspicious translucent shutters.

That's insane, Anna! Forget it! I tried to shove the thought out of my mind, but my gaze kept returning to the overgrown shrubbery. No one was around to see me walk up there. I was dead certain none of houses within half a block were inhabited except for the Halls' place down the street, and I'd be well out of their line of vision. I hadn't seen a car since the roofers left. If someone did happen to drive by, the darkness and the bushes would give me plenty of cover.

Telling myself I was totally out of my mind, I set my cell phone on vibrate and stuffed it into the pocket of my jeans, along with my car keys. It took me less than two seconds to slide out of my car, slip across the wide-open front yard, and press my body into the prickly bushes. I stood there for what seemed an eternity, catching my breath, listening, and scheming. If I didn't see anything through that window, I'd creep back to my car and hightail it home. In the morning, I'd call Underwood. Tell him my theory without admitting I'd ever left my car. But if I caught a glimpse of a flashlight or the flicker of a candle, I'd call 911 on the spot. I wasn't going to let Ben get away

I listened for any sound that didn't belong to the evening, but heard only the buzz of a mosquito. Ignoring the sharp claws of the branches, I inched along the edge of the bushes until I came opposite the long, shuttered window next door. I strained to pick out any signs of movement through the opaqueness, but couldn't. If I hoped to see anything at all, I'd have to leave the protection of the shrubbery.

No one's inside. Go back to your car. Such sensible advice I gave myself. Ignoring it, I left the cover of the bushes and made it to the window in four swift steps. To my dismay, my foot landed on the gravel walkway with a crunch that echoed into the dusk. I flattened myself against the concrete wall. It was cold and bare. If the kids were inside, had they heard me? I waited, not daring to move. But there were no sounds, no signs of human presence.

Don't push your luck. Get out of here. This is a wild goose chase. Still . . . I was so close. I crept to the window. The lowest glass pane had indeed been broken out, leaving jagged edges, and its fiberglass shutter was definitely inside the house, probably propped up on a window sill. I tried to peer in, but I couldn't see a thing.

I didn't quite know when I first began to hear the low rumble like distant thunder. My concentration had been so focused on the window that my awareness of the sound came gradually, like waking up and realizing the alarm has been screaming for awhile. By the time the rumble invaded my consciousness, it had become so deep it seemed to shake the ground beneath my feet. A hiss. A clank. Then a deep roar, getting closer and closer. In a flash of insight I recognized its source. A heavy truck. A very heavy truck. The Halls must be getting their roof tiles!

Before I could slip back to my car, I heard shouts and realized it was too late to move. Better just slip back to the bushes and wait there till they left.

The shouting, clanking, and roaring seemed endless as I took cover between two branches. A mosquito buzzed around my ears. I heard another truck approach, then more shouts and sharp crashes.

Suppose Ben and Rachel were in the house. What would they think about all this commotion? Would they move around, perhaps with flashlights or candles? The workers and trucks were all at the Halls' place. No one was anywhere near this side of the white house. Warily, I tiptoed back to its window, straining my eyes to pick up a sign of life inside. Nothing. I listened for human voices, but all I heard was the din of moving vehicles. From the sound, I guessed they were using lighter ones now–some sort of mobile forklifts probably. I pictured them running back and forth, moving the heavy concrete tiles to the Halls' yard, releasing load after load with claps like thunder.

Without warning, an extra sharp bang split the air, and I heard the crackle of shattering glass. As my shocked eyes followed the noise, I saw that a round hole had appeared in the fiberglass shutter just above the one I had been trying to peek through. Instinct took over. I dropped to the ground and covered my head with my arms.

Someone was shooting at me!

Chapter Twenty-four

Gravel dug into my bare skin as I snaked across the overgrown path toward the protective cover of the bushes. I barely noticed. Another sharp crack echoed through the night. Frantically, I inventoried my body for pain. Every muscle complained, but nothing felt like a bullet wound. Finally it dawned on me that what I'd heard wasn't a shot—not this time. It was only the roofers, continuing their work as if nothing had happened. They probably hadn't even noticed the gunshot amid their own clatter and banging. Flipping sideways. I rolled into the bushes and lay motionless on my stomach, listening.

Hearing nothing that sounded like human presence, I slowly raised myself to a half crouch and pressed my body into the unfriendly stiff branches. Cautiously, I edged sideways toward the front of the house. A thorn tackled my shirt, but I yanked free, heedless of ripping fabric and tearing skin.

When I reached the end of the shrubbery, I surveyed the wide-open front yard. The distance between me and my car wasn't large, but there was no cover at all. What to do? Yell for help? Who would hear over the roofers' racket? *Make a break for it. Now!* Thank God I hadn't locked my car door!

In one mad dash I reached my Focus, yanked open the door, and dove inside. Sliding as low in the driver's seat as I could, I started the engine, backed up the street to the nearest driveway, turned around, and took off in the opposite direction from the roofing trucks. As I raced toward civilization, I glanced over my shoulder every three seconds. No one was following me.

When I reached the relative safety of Route 41, I pulled into a well-lighted car lot, grabbed my cell phone, and punched 911. My voice quavered as I identified myself to the dispatcher. "Someone shot at me! The address is . . . ." I grabbed my notebook and read the house number on Linda Street by the light from my open glove compartment.

"Are you at that address now?"

"No, I got away. I'm at Palm Automotive on Route 41."

"The address you gave me—is that your house?"

"No, it's a deserted house. Storm damaged." I stopped, realizing how bizarre my story was sounding. It would get worse. "May I speak with Detective Underwood or Detective Domagala-either one?"

"They're not on duty."

Of course not. I steeled myself for the rash of questions I knew would follow. "I was watching that house because I thought the runaway teens, Ben Tolliver and Rachel York, might be holed up there. That's when someone shot at me."

There was a moment of silence. Then, "Repeat that, please." I did. "And you're at Palm?" asked the crisp female voice.

"Yes, in the parking lot."

"OK, stay there. An officer will come right away to talk to you."

"No, don't send anyone here. Send everyone to Linda Street!" Before the dispatcher could protest, I added, "I'll drive myself to the station. I'm not far away."

The interview room where I found myself a short time later triggered unpleasant memories and a sense of dread. My questioner, an officer named Larsen, pounded me with questions. My head ached, my voice turned puny, and my whole body felt like it was melting the way snow turns into a dirty puddle in the gutter.

"You're sure you heard a gunshot?" Larsen pressed. "You said the roofing trucks out front made a lot of racket. Could it have been backfire?"

I stared at him, mentally calculating his IQ. "A window exploded just above my head, and a round hole appeared in the shutter," I told him for the second or third time.

"Uh-huh," he said. "And why again were you standing in the dark, peeping through the window of a deserted house?"

A tap on the door saved me from answering this question one more time, and Detective Underwood burst into the room. "Hello again, Ms. Sebastian." Neither his voice nor his expression held a trace of friendliness. His pock-scarred forehead was strawberry red, his eyes angry.

"Did you find Ben?" I asked.

He shook his head darkly. "I want to know what happened." He crossed the room to face me up close, towering over me. "Take it from the top, and don't skip any details."

Underwood listened to my account without interrupting, his mouth a tight, thin line. When I finished, he said, "The bullet was buried in the wall above the bed. I'll have a report on it shortly. We found your tracks in front of the window and along the bushes next door. Some light blue cotton threads on a branch—I'm betting they match your blouse."

I turned to show him the rip in the back of my shirt sleeve.

"There's a line of overgrown juniper along the back of the lot, and we found a place where it had been tromped down pretty good." His eyes flashed. "Your gunman wasn't over six yards from where you were standing."

He paused to let that sink in, and I wondered if he could see the goose bumps crawling up my arms as he continued. "The shot went through the second pane up. It was over your head, but not that far. Either someone was trying to scare you off or their aim was high. You're a mighty lucky lady." His tone said "mighty lucky *stupid* lady."

"Then who—?" I didn't know where to go with this sentence so I just sat there, trying to read his face.

"Best guess? Your teenager slipped out the back door—other side of the house from where you were standing—crept up a row of hibiscus between him and the yard beyond, then followed the line of juniper across the back to the mashed place we found."

"Ben ?" *Not Ben!*

"Oh, those kids were there all right–or at least someone was. They left dirty dishes and towels all over the place, and probably plenty of fingerprints too. Like I said, the shooter might just have been trying to chase you off."

I struggled to take it all in. "But how would Ben get a gun?" Neither Tiffany nor Gordy had said anything about a gun missing from their trailer.

"Whoever lived in that house kept revolvers in shoe boxes in the bedroom closet, and one of the boxes was empty. We'll track down the owner, of course, check if one's missing."

"But how did Ben know I was there?" As soon as the words passed my lips, I recognized what should have been obvious all along. "I guess he and Rachel were looking out the front window." In my mind, I pictured two surprised teenagers standing in the dark kitchen, watching me through translucent storm shutters. I could imagine the expression on their faces as they saw me park in front of the house next door, cross the street to speak to the construction workers, return to my car, and eventually dash across the front yard to the overgrown bushes between the houses.

"The kids got away before we arrived," Underwood said, "thanks to the very ample warning you gave them." He looked at me as if I were road kill. "In spite of what you think of our investigative skills, Ms. Sebastian, your Police Department had already identified that place as a possible hideout. We were getting ready to set up some surveillance on five houses, including that one. We would have spotted the runaways, and we'd have gone in with enough resources to keep them from escaping." He strode to the door, then turned back toward me. "So thanks a lot for your help." To Larsen, he said, "I'm finished with this witness." He slammed the door behind him.

Chapter Twenty-five

After Underwood finally finished interrogating me, I treated myself to a real bath in Mother's olive green tub and fell into bed. But I tossed and turned, and when at last I slept, I had a nightmare. I was fleeing from a faceless pursuer in something like tapioca pudding. He shot at me, and the crack of gunfire woke me up.

I sat up. I had dreamed the noise, hadn't I?

The night was silent now, but the echo of the shot still rang in my ears. It felt real.

I checked the lighted numbers on the clock beside my bed. 1:29 a.m.

I turned on the bed lamp. Still shaky, I dangled my feet off the edge of the mattress for what seemed like a good ten minutes, my ears attune to the slightest sound. Nothing. I'd had a bad dream, that's all.

I got up and made my way to the kitchen, turning on lights as I went. I checked the front and back doors—both securely locked—and opened the door between the garage and the house. I never bothered to lock that one, but my squeaky old garage door was securely down, and it couldn't have opened without my hearing it. Slowly, I walked through every room. Nothing seemed disturbed. Returning to the kitchen, I poured myself a glass of milk and let my heartbeat slow to something closer to its normal rate. I'd just had a nightmare. My subconscious was processing the shock of last night's events.

Back to bed. But halfway down the hall, I stopped. Prickles like a thousand ants started up my spine. My bedroom door was half closed. I was sure I'd left it open. Cautiously, I nudged it back until it hit the doorstop. No one jumped out from behind it. Conscious of the thumping in my chest, I surveyed the room. No armed intruder stood there ready to pounce. The door had probably just caught a draft when the air conditioner came on. But as I entered the room, I couldn't shake the feeling that something wasn't quite right.

Suddenly I knew what it was. I hadn't felt my purse on the doorknob where I usually hung it. A quick glance confirmed my suspicion. It wasn't there.

Of course, my handbag didn't really belong on the doorknob; it had a proper place on my closet shelf. Most of the time, however, I just dropped it over the knob as I came into the bedroom. Did I actually put it away last night? I must have. If I'd left it anywhere else in the house, I would have spotted it when I checked all the rooms. I didn't recall putting it in the closet, but then I didn't remember hanging it on the doorknob either. I'd been too preoccupied with everything that happened in the last few hours. My purse was probably right there on my closet shelf. Still, I knew I wouldn't sleep until I'd laid eyes on it. Chiding myself for my paranoia, I marched to my closet and flung open its bifold door.

For the moment it took a scream to form in my throat, I stared at the figure who stood framed in the opening. My purse hung over his shoulder and a gun trembled in his hand. I shrieked his name.

"Ben!"

"Thanks for the ride, Anna," he said. Then he lunged. And everything went black.

Chapter Twenty-six

"Anna?" The voice seemed to come from the bottom of a deep well. "Anna!"

No, I must be the one in the well. The speaker was above me. My eyelids came unstuck and a familiar face came fuzzily into focus. "What are you doing here, Dr. Jo?" I mumbled.

"The ER doctor called me. I'm sorry to wake you."

"Oh." I closed my eyes again, gradually becoming aware of the whiteness of my surroundings and the backdrop of beeps and hums. "What time is it?"

"7:30," he said. Then he added gently, "7:30 Wednesday morning."

"I must have slept," I said, stating the obvious.

"And that's good. You took a bad blow on the head. I hear you had an unexpected visitor."

"You know about it then." I felt relieved that I didn't have to go through the whole grisly story again.

"I know enough."

Agonizing memories returned. Finding Ben in my closet. Crashing to my bedroom floor. My throbbing head. Paramedics and police appearing like angels before I'd even figured out if I could move. The ambulance ride to Fawcett Hospital. The seemingly endless hours of waiting in the ER, interspersed with bursts of frenetic activity. I had been punctured, prodded, questioned, X-rayed, and CT-scanned. Then around five, miracle of miracles, the white and green-coated figures left me alone in my curtained cubicle. I closed my eyes gratefully. Now the morning I'd thought I might never see had actually arrived.

"How do you feel?" Dr. Jo asked.

I checked my body parts one at a time. Toes wiggled. Feet waggled. Legs moved and bent appropriately at the knees. My left shoulder hurt. World War III waged inside my head, but not as fiercely as it had last night. The throbbing had stopped, and my vision was clear. "Not too bad, I guess. Considering."

"The 911 caller said you were unconscious. Do you have any idea how long you were out?"

His question surprised me—not the part about losing consciousness—people had been asking me that all night. It was the part about the caller. "Do you know who contacted 911?" Last night, I hadn't even asked. Too groggy, I guess.

"According to the detective out there in the waiting room, they got an anonymous call, but they traced it to your house. The caller said you were unconscious."

"My house?" Only one person could have called from my house. Waves of emotion hit me, one after the other. Shock. Anger. Frustration. Sadness. And finally gratitude. Ben didn't have to call; in fact, it was plain stupid.

Dr. Jo repeated his question. "Do you know how long you were unconscious?"

"I don't think it was very long."

"The detective said your assailant had a gun. Did he hit you with it?"

"No, he tackled me." *His coach would have been proud,* I thought with a flash of irony. "Apparently I hit my head on the footboard of my bed when I went down." When the doctor didn't say anything, I added, "He stole my car—did you know that? I guess he got the keys from my purse. He stole that too."

Dr. Jo nodded with a sympathetic grunt. "What makes you think you weren't out long?"

"I heard my car pulling out of the garage. And I'm sure he didn't waste any time getting out of there." *Except to call 911.*

"The paramedics said you were conscious when they arrived, but still on the floor."

"Yeah, I just lay there for a bit, trying to decide if anything was broken and wondering if I'd pass out if I tried to get to the phone. Then the paramedics arrived and made all my decisions for me."

"Thank God!"

No. Thank Ben.

Holding up two fingers, he asked, "How many fingers do you see?" After I answered to his apparent satisfaction, he checked my eyes with a light, listened to my heart, and prodded various body parts asking if they hurt.

"Excellent," he pronounced. Apparently the places that made me flinch weren't the critical ones. "The X-rays don't show any broken bones. CT-scan doesn't indicate anything unusual either. I predict you'll be good as new, but it's going to take a few days." He rubbed his chin thoughtfully. "I'm trying to decide what to do here. Medically, I could release you from the ER later in the morning if you don't develop nausea or dizziness. But I have a notion to admit you to the hospital just to make sure you rest for a day or two." To my surprise, my doctor leaned against the edge of my bed and spoke very gently. "This thing with the two boys has hit you hard, Anna, and you were already carrying the burden of your mother's illness."

The obvious concern in his kind face brought a lump to my throat. "I'm OK. Really. And I want to go home."

"If I release you, I want you to take the rest of the week off. Don't show up at the office before Monday unless you come to see me as your doctor, not your boss, OK? I think we can manage without you till then." With a smile, he added, "Though it may be hard."

I felt tears well up. "Thank you, Doctor Jo. Thanks for everything."

He patted my good shoulder and stood. "I'll order you some breakfast, and I'll check on you later in the morning. If your food settles and you still don't have any symptoms of concussion, I'll let you go. One of the gals in our practice has already volunteered to drive you home."　He started toward the white curtains that surrounded me, then stopped and turned back. "That police detective out there wants to talk to you, but I can tell him you won't be up to it till later."

"What's his name?"

"Underwood."

"I better see him now," I said with a sigh.

Chapter Twenty-seven

Peering at me over the foot of my hospital bed, Detective Underwood looked like he hadn't slept for weeks. "How are you feeling?" he asked.

It wasn't the warmest greeting I'd ever received, but at least he didn't seem as furious with me as he had last night. "Stupid," I said. "Ben must have hidden in my back seat while I was out peeking in his window. And I drove him straight into my garage. Stupid, stupid, stupid."

"And he got away again," he said, making me feel even worse. After a long pause, he added, "In your car."

"I hope he figures out how to drive before he totals it."

"Well, if it's any consolation, we found your purse on your washing machine. Doesn't look like he took anything but your car keys and your cash."

Amazement and relief washed over me. At least I wouldn't have to deal with a missing driver's license and credit cards. "There wasn't much money in it. Not over twenty dollars."

"Good. And the doc says you'll recover." He didn't sound overly happy about that. "Lucky again," he added, moving as close to the head of my bed as was practical, given the array of machines I was attached to. "I'd like to hear your version of the story. Are you up to that?"

"Much as I'll ever be, I guess."

He listened poker-faced as I filled him in on the details. When I came to the part about finding Ben in my closet, he interrupted. "He had a gun?"

"Yes. He could have shot me—or hit me with it, but he didn't. He just said, 'Thanks for the ride.' Then he tackled me." A sudden thought struck me. "About what happened at their hideout, how could Ben have been out back shooting at me at the same time he must have been sneaking into my car? That doesn't add up."

Shaking his head slowly, Underwood said, "No, it doesn't."

"And what about Rachel? Did she duck down in my back seat along with Ben? It's not a very big car. Did they both stay hidden in it all the while I was parked at the police station? And did Rachel wait in my garage while Ben snuck in to steal my car keys?"

"No." He stretched it into a two-syllable word. "I don't think so." He parted the white curtains at the end of my bed and stuck his head out. Apparently satisfied that the whole world wasn't eavesdropping on our conversation, he maneuvered his way around my IV pole and spoke quietly. "We're going to release this information to the press today anyway, so I might as well fill you in." Catching my look, he quickly added, "Don't worry, we won't mention your name, but we need to put out the word that Ben Tolliver was spotted in Port Charlotte." His eyes locked with mine. "And that Rachel York was not with him." He glanced at the IV bag going drip, drip, drip into my veins. "Young Tolliver's fingerprints were all over the hideout," he said, "but we didn't find any of the girl's."

Stunned, I said, "She wasn't there? Her note said she going to join Ben."

"Which leads us to believe she didn't write that note of her own free will."

I opened my mouth to tell him he must be wrong, but snapped it shut when something Candy Owen told me flashed through my mind. *Rachel ended her note with "I love you." She never said that before.* Could someone have dictated those words? Or did she write them as a desperate signal that something was amiss? Looking up at Underwood, I asked, "So you're thinking—?"

"We're thinking there's a good chance the girl was abducted and that she was forced to write the note as a ploy."

Abducted! "Ben wouldn't do that."

"No." Underwood pulled out a handkerchief and wiped his brow. "No, he wouldn't. Couldn't, even. And it's obvious he didn't take the bus to Fort Myers either. The girl might have."

"But the ticket agent said someone was with her—a male."

"Could have been her abductor. He could have forced her to buy two tickets to Fort Myers—again to throw us off the track. Or the agent could have been wrong about recognizing Rachel's picture."

I tried to shut out the monstrous images that were pushing their way into my mind. "Do you think she's still alive?" I whispered.

"Sure hope so." Even as I watched Underwood mop his forehead, I felt cold all over and tugged my hospital blanket closer to my chin. "Our best hope is that the perp took her as a hostage," he said.

"Hostage?"

"Bait."

As his implication hit, my body convulsed in a shudder. "Bait to catch Ben?" It wasn't a question really, but I couldn't make myself speak it as fact.

"If Ben Tolliver didn't kill his brother, then he sure as hell knows who did. And that person wants to find him—real bad— before we do." He waited for me to absorb this before he added, "That has to be the reason he shot at you last night."

It took a minute for this to register. "Jessie's killer . . . that's who shot at me?"

"Think about it."

I was. I couldn't stop thinking about it!

Underwood went on. "Picture this. The killer has finally found Ben's hideout, and there you are looking in the window. He can't afford to let you call in the police before he's had a chance to get to the kid. He has to scare you off. Or kill you."

A shrill alarm sounded, making me practically leap out of my bed. Underwood darted out of my cubicle and returned a minute later with a nurse. She adjusted one of the machines and hurried out again. The detective closed the curtains behind her before he continued. "The shooter probably found his way into the house the minute you drove off. The back door was standing wide open when our team got there, and I doubt the boy left it that way."

"But how would this guy have found the hideout?"

"Maybe he tracked it down the same way you did. More likely he followed you."

"No! No one followed me. I looked a hundred times!"

"The way you were systematically cris-crossing streets, it wouldn't take a brain surgeon to figure out what you were doing. And if it was your boyfriend, he probably recognized your car."

"Jack Braxton is not my boyfriend."

"Sorry," he said, not sounding it. "Anyway, whoever it was wouldn't have needed to stick right behind you; he'd just drive by on a cross street occasionally, see if you stopped somewhere."

And I'd played right into his hand, leaving my car conspicuously parked on Linda Street while I talked with everybody on the block. I shut my eyes, trying to shut out the accusation on Underwood's face. It didn't help. The inner pictures were even worse. When I looked up, I found the detective staring at me as if he could X-ray my thoughts.

"What about Tiffany?" I asked him. Do you know yet what caused her death?"

"So far it looks like suicide. We found an empty Xanax bottle in the medicine cabinet, prescribed the day before. I suppose her doctor was trying to help her cope with her son's murder, but he should have known better. She must have taken the whole bottle."

"That's what killed her?"

"Not by itself. An unlabeled drug container on the kitchen counter showed traces of crushed Oxycontin. Idiot dopeheads smash the pills to get the full kick all at once, you know? The combination seems to be the cause of death, though we don't have the full report yet."

Suicide. Or an accidental drug overdose. That meant . . . . "Then Jack didn't kill her."

Underwood rubbed his left temple, and I noticed how tired he looked. "We tracked down the license number of the silver Toyota Camry the Tollivers' neighbor saw parked in front of the trailer around the time she died. It's registered to Braxton's backyard neighbor who just happens to be up north till after January. We got hold of the owner up in Oshkosh. Seems he left a key with his good neighbor Mr. Braxton, who had offered to watch over the house while he was away."

Underwood gave me a long, hard look "We didn't find Braxton's fingerprints inside the trailer, but there were plenty on the outside of the door. Not enough evidence to prove he had a hand in her death, but it's a mighty damn big coincidence."

Chapter Twenty-eight

Dr. Johansen sprung me from the ER a little before ten, and the gracious woman who works insurance claims in our medical practice drove me to Enterprise, where I rented a car. When I got home, I inspected every room in the house, shining a flashlight under my bed, punching the clothes in the closets, peeking behind the shower curtains, and double-checking all the windows. Locking the barn door.

I called Kate, who could barely believe all that had happened since I'd left her house last night. "Rest well," she told me as we said goodbye.

Rest. How exactly does one rest with every muscle screaming and every nerve fiber jangling? Dr. Jo had offered pills, but I declined, telling him I'd be fine once I got home. But I wasn't fine.

I collapsed into Mother's recliner in the living room and picked up a novel I'd wanted to read. I couldn't concentrate. I kept thinking about everything Underwood had told me. Rachel wasn't with Ben. She had probably been abducted by someone who wanted to use her as bait to catch Ben. Was Jack that someone? Underwood thought he was. Did I?

My mind flashed back to our dinner at his house—before he transformed into a total stranger. Over and over, Jack had asked me what I knew about Ben. Did I have any idea where he and Rachel could be? Did Ben have any friends the police might have overlooked? Did Rachel?

As I thought back on our conversation, I became more and more certain that Jack had been desperate to find Ben. Underwood's words played through my mind. *If Ben didn't kill his brother, he sure as hell knows who did. And the killer wants real bad to find him before we do.*

Jack knew how much Ben cared about Rachel, so he'd expect Ben to fall for a trap that used the girl as bait. Jack was a Georgia Bulldog, and someone called Bulldog was the villain in Ben's poem. Besides all that, Jack had been at Tiffany's trailer close to the time she died. I couldn't imagine what Tiffany's death could have to do with Jessie's murder, but I had a gnawing feeling it fit somewhere.

Everything pointed to Jack as Jessie's killer. Didn't it?

I rocked back and forth, staring at the book in front of me without seeing the words. Something nagged at me. Something didn't quite fit into the picture that was trying to take shape in my brain. Suddenly I knew what it was. Ben's poems! If Jack was the Bulldog in *Forsaken Angel,* the poem Ben wrote about Jessie's death, why hadn't he referred to Jack as Bulldog in his earlier poems? A line from *First Down* ran through my mind. *"Good catch," says Coach."* Coach, not Bulldog.

I set my novel down on the coffee table and thought more about *Forsaken Angel.* There was something eerie about a fifteen-year-old boy who was so schooled in secrecy that he had to cloak any mention of his brother's death in elaborate images. A forsaken angel, guilty of nothing, punished forever. A city swarmed by mad dogs, including the dangerous Bulldog. I was sure Jessie was the forsaken angel who fell into the water. And Jack was probably Bulldog, Jessie's killer. Ben had written that poem at Jack's house. Still, I could never recall hearing Ben call his coach Bulldog.

Besides, Ben had been writing about vicious dogs before he even knew Jack.

The dogs that swarmed the city in Ben's last poem seemed to be the same dogs that howled and broke down gates in *The Dark,* the poem Ben gave me back when he still lived with the Owens. Kate had convinced me that the dogs in both poems referred to the biblical book of *Revelation* where dogs symbolized the evil-doers who were supposed to be locked outside the gates of heaven. When

Ben gave me *The Dark* so many months ago, I'd suspected that the dogs represented the drug scene. What if I'd been right?

In spite of all her clean drug screens, Tiffany had gotten hold of Oxycontin somewhere. That suggested the possibility that she'd been using drugs all along. The pros had a variety of ways to cheat the required tests, and Tiffany had enough history of substance abuse to qualify as a pro. Could the driver of the BMW Vera Mosely saw at the trailer possibly be a dealer from the past who had recently reappeared? Could that explain Ben's line, *Bulldog bares his teeth then and now?*

Oh, yuk! I'd been over every bit of this before like a cow chewing its cud. I wasn't making progress; I was just making myself sick. In frustration, I picked up my novel and tried to focus on it. I had resolutely turned over three pages when the rest of the line I'd remembered from Ben's football poem floated into my head. *"Good catch," says Coach. "Nice job." Wish Mama was here.*

Mama. I had assumed Mama was Ben's mother. But no! Mama was his grandmother. Tiffany's mother! It was "Mama" who gave him the little stuffed toy he took with him when he ran away—the black and white dog he called Floyd. It was Mama who taught him about the Bible. It was Mama who appeared in his poetry after she was no longer with him in the flesh. Not his mother, his grandmother.

Whatever became of the grandmother Ben called Mama? The only thing I could remember reading about Tiffany's mother was that she was deceased. Suddenly curious, I abandoned my novel, grabbed the Tolliver case file from the shelf in my study, and carried it to the kitchen table.

Any information I had about Tiffany's dead mother would be buried in the records that had been transferred from other counties. When I'd first been assigned to the case, I had read through these old documents, which were stored in the DCF office. Now I thumbed through my case file, hunting the notes I had taken. Found them. On top of my handwritten pages, I had stapled a brief chronology.

March 1998. Ben (age 9) and Jessie (age 6) removed from parents' in Fort Myers, Florida, on allegations of drug abuse and neglect. Placed in custody of paternal grandmother.

July '98. Paternal grandmother stated she "could not handle the boys." Placed in foster care.

Nov. '98. Children returned to Mother after she graduated from a drug rehab program. Parents had separated.

Feb. '99. Tiffany and boys moved with a boyfriend named Otis Epps to Broward County after bank foreclosed on Tiffany's condo in Ft. Myers.

Nov. '99. Ben (age 10) caught stealing food from Publix. Indications of drug abuse, neglect. Children taken back into foster care.

Nov. '99. March '03. Records sketchy. Boys lived in at least 5 foster homes.

March '03. Children again reunited with their mother.

May '03. Tiffany and boys moved to Punta Gorda with a boyfriend, Greg Olner.

Sept. '03. Children removed from home, allegations of neglect and mother's drug abuse. Placed in foster care with George and Candy Owen, Punta Gorda, Florida.

That's when I entered the case, just over a year ago.

As I studied the chronology, I wondered why the judge had awarded custody to Gordy's mother back in '98 when the children first became dependents of the court. Why not to Mama, Tiffany's mother, with whom Ben seemed to have such a close relationship? Had Mama died by that time?

I shuffled through my notes. The first mention of maternal grandparents came in November 1999 in the earliest records from Broward County. Yes, here it was. The Protective Investigator, justifying her decision to place the children in foster care, had noted:

No available relatives. Father's whereabouts unknown. Maternal grandparents deceased, paternal grandmother unwilling to take children.

When did Tiffany's mother die? I scanned my handwritten pages again, but found no other mention of a maternal grandmother. That seemed strange. "Mama" had been an important figure in Ben's early life. I reread the chronology. Paused at February '99. *Tiffany and boys moved with a boyfriend named Otis Epps to Broward County after bank foreclosed on Tiffany's condo in Ft. Myers.*

The bank foreclosed? That meant Tiffany had once held a mortgage on a condo. Gordy obviously wasn't in the picture at the time, so it wasn't likely he had purchased the condo. How did this single mother who had never held a more lucrative job than serving burgers at McDonald's manage to get that kind of financing?

Maybe she didn't. Maybe she inherited the condo after her mother died!

Yesterday morning, when I'd asked Ben's parents where their son had learned so much about the Bible, Tiffany told me the family had lived with her mother for awhile when the children were young. And my chronology indicated they hadn't come to DCF's attention until March 1998, when Ben would have been nine. Yet Tiffany had given birth to a son with Fetal Alcohol Syndrome six years before that, so she hadn't exactly been a stable parent during those early years. Had Mama, in fact, been the primary caregiver—perhaps until her death? That could explain why no problems were reported earlier. And if Mama had become closely attached to her grandchildren, it made sense that she would leave her condo to their mother.

I flipped back through my notes to check where Tiffany and the children lived back in '98 when DCF first became involved in their lives. Yes! I had copied down a street and number. If my speculation that Tiffany inherited a condo from her mother was correct, could this be its address? It was located in Fort Myers. Less than an hour away. It seemed possible—just barely possible—that someone in the same building would remember the Tolliver family. If Tiffany was into drugs back then, someone just might recall a visitor nicknamed Bulldog.

It was a long shot. And I had promised Dr. Jo I would rest. But my headache was gone, and my shoulder only hurt when I moved it the wrong way. I was too charged up to sleep. A drive to Fort Myers could be restful, couldn't it? At least I wouldn't be crawling through bushes getting shot at! And I'd be back in time to take a good nap.

I packed a peanut butter sandwich to eat in the car. Then I spread a Fort Myers map on the kitchen counter and planned my route.

Chapter Twenty-nine

The condo where Tiffany Tolliver and her children had once lived was located in a complex of dingy two-story buildings that lacked playgrounds, ball fields, and tenants under seventy. I parked in a "guest" spot and climbed the steps to a covered walkway. Squinting at numbers on the doors, I found 237 and knocked.

I introduced myself to the white-haired, gray-faced woman who answered. "I'm looking for someone who knew a family that lived in this condo in the late nineties—the Tollivers."

Glancing from my face to the badge that hung like a lanyard around my neck, she asked, "You a social worker or something?"

"Something like that," I fudged. "I'm a Guardian Ad Litem, working with the Tolliver family."

The woman nodded as if she understood what that meant though I doubted she did. "Only been here two years," she said.

"Are there any old-timers around, anyone who might have known the folks who lived here before you?"

The woman adjusted her glasses to get a better look at my badge. "Rosemary Irving, down the hall, been here a right long time. I think she maybe knew the folks lived here. Apartment 241. You might could try her."

Rosemary Irving, in 241, answered my knock with a friendly smile. Although she was probably no younger than her neighbor, she was better nourished and seemed farther away from the grave. I introduced myself. "I'm looking for someone who knew the family who used to live in Apartment 237, two doors down. I don't know the owner's name, but she had a daughter named Tiffany."

Her eyes lit up. "Land sakes, yes, I knew Lillian. Still miss her."

"And you knew her daughter Tiffany?" Sensing the woman's hesitation, I quickly explained that I was a Guardian Ad Litem, working with the Tolliver children.

Rosemary frowned. "Guardian? Something happen to Tiffany?"

"Oh, I'm not a guardian in that sense." Carefully avoiding her question about Tiffany, I said, "The family has come under the protection of the Charlotte County Court. I represent the children's interests during the legal proceedings."

The woman locked eyes with mine and drew her mouth into a thin line. "In trouble again, huh?" With a huge sigh, she swung the door wide. "Well, you better come on in."

"Thank you, Ms. Irving."

"Call me Rosemary."

Rosemary ushered me to a seat on a flowered couch in her neat but faded living room. "I'm not surprised DCF's on her tail again," she said as she sank into a wingback chair across from me. "That little brainless tramp ought to never had kids. Don't know what they'd of done without Lillian—not that they ever said 'thank you.'" She folded her arms over her chest. "Lillian was more mother to those kids than that daughter of hers ever thought of being."

So I'd guessed right. "The family lived here with Lillian for a time?"

Rosemary snorted. "For a long time. The oldest boy, Benny, wasn't even two when his mother come crying to Lillian. And she took them in. Ever once in awhile, that good-for-nothing Gordy showed up like God's greatest gift, and Lillian always took him in, don't ask me why. He'd smile his big, toothy smile, talking about some pie-in-the-sky scheme. He was a charmer, you know. Could make you believe anything, first couple times anyway. Off he'd go to make his fortune, taking the family with him. But the pie in the sky always turned to sour pudding, and before long they'd come whining back with some sorry tale. He never held a real job for long."

"Was he into drugs?"

"Huh! Lillian turned a blind eye—said they just drank a bit too much. Well, they drank a lot more than a bit too much, and they were into other stuff too. Whatever they could get, you know? I told Lil she should throw them out—them and their dopehead friends that kept coming around." Rosemary shook her head, seeming to gaze at something far away. "She just couldn't turn her back on those grandkids."

I took a deep breath. "What happened to Lillian?"

"Oh, Lord, she got cancer. Pancreas." Pain played over her round face, and she closed her eyes for a moment. When she opened them, she spoke softly. "She didn't last six months after they found it, and they say that's what killed her but . . . ." Her voice trailed off.

"But what?"

"But she started going downhill after the little boy died. And then they went and took her other kids away. Maybe the cancer had something to do with it, but I think she died of a broken heart."

I gripped the arm of the couch. "What little boy?"

"Little Leon." She titled her head questioningly. "Surely you know about Leon?"

"No!"

"He was only three, and he had all kinds of problems. Lil told me it was because Tiffany drank too much while she was carrying him."

I felt my jaw tighten. Another baby born with fetal alcohol syndrome.

"Leon never learned to talk. And he had epilepsy—bad. But Lil loved him. She called him her little angel."

Epilepsy! So Kate had been right about Ben's poem. Only the "angel who fell into fire and water" wasn't Jessie. It was Leon!

Collecting my composure, I asked, "How did Leon die?"

"Heart attack during a seizure."

An involuntary gasp slipped from my lips, interrupting Rosemary's story, but after a moment she continued. "The doctor had warned them he had a weak heart, but it was still an awful shock. I felt sorry for them all, especially Lillian. She and her daughter had gone out shopping, and Gordy was watching the kids—it was one of those spells when he was around. When Lil and Tiffany got home, they saw the ambulance parked in front. Gordy tried CPR, but he couldn't save his son. Lillian never got over it."

For a stunned moment, I could only shake my head. Finally I managed to ask, "How old was Ben when this happened?"

Rosemary frowned. "I think he was about three years older than Jessie, and Jessie was about two years older than Leon. And Leon was three."

I did the arithmetic. "So Ben would have been about eight."

"Sounds right."

I tried to imagine the effect of losing a younger brother on an eight-year-old boy. I couldn't.

"Rosemary," I said slowly, "you said Lillian called Leon her 'little angel.' Did you ever hear her refer to him as a 'forsaken angel'?"

Rosemary stared at me as if she'd seen a ghost. "How do you know that?"

"Ben writes poetry. He's quite gifted, actually. And the title of one of his poems is 'Forsaken Angel.'"

Rosemary lowered her head into her hands. When at last she looked up, she wiped away tears. "Lillian used to be very religious," she said, her voice cracking. "She had a Bible quote for nearly everything. When she'd tell me about the latest horrible thing that happened with Tiffany or Gordy, she would always add, 'but God promises he will never forsake us.' Until Leon died. A couple weeks after that happened, she told me, 'The Lord did forsake his little angel.' I think Leon's death really shook her faith. Ever after that, when she'd talk about that little boy, she'd call him 'my poor little lost lamb' or 'my little forsaken angel.'"

The lamb is abandoned, the angel forsaken. Darkness overcomes. So Ben's first poem was about Leon too!

We sat lost in the darkness of our own thoughts until finally I broke the silence. "Earlier you mentioned that someone took the other children away after Leon died."

Rosemary nodded sadly. "Just a few months later. Gordy got some kind of bug up his ass about Lillian. Maybe he thought she blamed him for not saving Leon, I don't know. Anyway, one day he packed up and moved in with his mother. Then he decided he wanted his boys." She gave me a disgusted look. "Well, I'm not sure he really *wanted* them, but they was his rightful property, you know. Anyway, he called DCF claiming Tiffany was on drugs and Lillian was mentally ill."

Dumbstruck, I tried to make the picture of Ben's father square with the friendly, cooperative Gordy Tolliver I had always liked. Of course he'd been on drugs himself then. That could explain the radical change in personality. "What happened then?" I asked.

"After Gordy called, DCF sent investigators over to check, and they up and decided none of them was fit to raise the kids. They figured out real quick Tiffany and Gordy was both on drugs. And they said Lillian knowingly let them use stuff in the children's presence, which I guess she did, but what was she supposed to do? She was just trying to take care of her grandkids, and she sure wasn't mentally ill. Oh, she took pills for anxiety—had a panic attack once in a moon—but she wasn't sick in the head. Not a bit. Those investigators, though, they took the boys away and handed them to Gordy's mother, who didn't know billy beans about raising young'uns—hardly even visited them when they was here."

So I'd been right that Mama had been the children's primary caregiver the first nine years of Ben's life. The DCF files hadn't mentioned that the family was still living with her when custody was given to Gordy's mother, but that was no surprise. Those early files that had been transferred through two other counties were mighty sparse.

Rosemary choked up again—whether from anger or sadness, I couldn't tell. But she quickly regained control and continued. "Gordy's mother only kept Ben and Jessie a few months before she admitted she couldn't handle them. Truth tell, I think she only asked for them out of meanness in the first place—to take them away from Lillian. But by the time she gave them up, Lillian had been diagnosed with cancer, so DCF wouldn't let her have the children. Jessie and Ben went to foster care, and Lil never saw them again." Rosemary swiped at her cheeks. "She passed a few months later. Like I told you, the doctors said the cancer got her, but I think she died of a broken heart."

I felt close to tears myself, but there were still things I wanted to know. "Tiffany lived in her mother's place for awhile after that, didn't she?"

"Yeah. Lil left her the condo, not that she deserved it."

"What about Gordy?"

"After his mom gave up the boys, he took off. Tiffany wasn't speaking to him, and he heard about another pie-in-the-sky scheme somewhere. Tiffany though—she cleaned up her act for awhile. She graduated from a drug program and stayed clean long enough to get her kids back. But then the bank foreclosed, and she moved in with another guy—even though she was still married to Gordy, mind you. After a few months, the boyfriend packed them all up and moved them over to Broward County. I think Tiffany was running from Lee County DCF." She met my eyes. "I sure felt sorry for those little boys."

I picked up my purse, signaling that it was time to bring our conversation to a close. "You've been so helpful, Rosemary. I just have one more question." It was a long shot, but I had to ask. "Did Lillian or Tiffany ever mention anyone called Bulldog?"

She frowned. "It sounds a little familiar, but I don't rightly know why."

"You said there were dopeheads around. Could one of them have been nicknamed Bulldog?"

Shaking her head slowly, Rosemary said, "Could be, I guess, but I honestly can't say. My memory ain't what it used to be, Honey."

Chapter Thirty

I got home around three with plenty of time for a nap before dinner. I took two Tylenol, fell into bed, and sank instantly into a deep sleep. Forty-five minutes later, however, I woke with memories of the last twenty-four hours swirling in my head. I'd been shot at. Tackled. Relieved of my car. Hospitalized. And shocked to the bone by Rosemary's story about little Leon Tolliver. My body felt like it shouldn't move, but my mind wouldn't be still. So much for resting.

Not knowing what else to do, I got up and called Kate. I needed the sound of a sympathetic voice. "You guessed right about epilepsy," I told her after the church secretary transferred my call, "only it wasn't Jessie who had it. Ben and Jessie had a younger brother who died during a seizure when Ben was eight." I gave her a quick version of my visit with the neighbor who'd been friends with the grandmother Ben called "Mama."

After we'd hashed over the details at least a dozen times, Kate said, "Try to stop thinking about it. The police are on it. There's nothing more you can do. Get some rest."

She was right, of course. Anyway, my brain was mush. I decided to check my email, more as a distraction than from any expectation of finding anything interesting. As I sat down at my computer, my gaze fell upon Mom's daisy-covered thermos next to my keyboard. Coffee! That's what I needed! But when I picked up the thermos to refill it, it rattled. Surprised, I shook it. There was no mistaking the telltale sound of broken glass. I opened it and stared into a black hole where the silver thermal lining should have been.

When did that happen? I hadn't used the thermos for a couple days, and I definitely hadn't dropped it. Perplexed, I looked around to see if anything else had been disturbed. Several months ago, when I'd converted my mother's guestroom to a computer area for myself, I'd pulled up the rancid, gold shag rug and to my delight found glistening white ceramic tile beneath it. Now my eyes focused on a black chip in that tile. That was new. And it was right where the coffee thermos would have landed if I had accidentally knocked it off my desktop.

Only I hadn't done that. It wasn't the kind of thing I'd forget. Leaning back in my rolling chair, I studied the shattered thermos. If I didn't knock it to the floor, who did?

Only one person besides me had been in my house.

I remembered waking with a start in the wee hours this morning, dreaming that I'd heard a gunshot. Even wide awake, I'd remained convinced I'd heard a real noise. A noise like the crash of a thermos striking the ceramic tile floor? Maybe. Someone who wasn't used to its presence at my work station could easily have bumped it with an elbow, especially if he hadn't turned on any lights.

Ben.

Shutting my eyes in concentration, I began fitting the pieces together. I pictured Ben tip-toeing into my house from the garage where he'd holed up on the floor of my car. He probably searched for my purse first—he needed my car keys. After he found it on the handle of my bedroom door and saw that I was sound asleep, he could have taken the opportunity to use my computer. Suppose he did. Suppose he accidentally knocked over the thermos in the dark. And the crash woke me. I remembered getting up and turning on lights, one after another. He must have slipped into my bedroom and hidden in my closet while I searched the rest of the house.

Opening my eyes, I frowned at my computer. What was important enough to cause Ben to risk taking the time to use it? Did he send a message? Or receive one—maybe from Rachel? I hit the shift key and waited for the screen to come to life.

I studied the list of messages in my Inbox, not expecting to find what I was looking for, but checking anyway. There was nothing I didn't recognize. Nothing in the Outbox. Or Sent items. Or Deleted items. Nothing unusual.

Of course not. Ben would have used Hotmail, and I couldn't get into his account unless I could somehow figure out his User Name and Password. That seemed hopeless, but I had to try.

Google took me to the Hotmail site, and for the User Name, I typed in *BenTolliver*. What password would he choose? Probably something that held significance for him. I tried *Rachel*. Got an error message. I tried *RachelYork*. Same nasty message. I tried Ben's birthday in every combination I could think of. More errors. I'd have to pull a miracle out of thin air.

Resting my forehead in my hands, I willed that miracle to pop into my brain. A few minutes later, I found my mind replaying my first interview with Detective Underwood. He'd asked me about Ben's poem—the one I'd discovered under the mattress in Jack's guest room. The detective had seemed surprised that the troubled teen wrote poetry, and I assured him Ben had a gift for it. "I used to call him Edgar Allen Tolliver," I'd told him. Underwood had smiled at that and muttered "Figures."

What figured? On a whim, I typed *EdgarAllen* into the Password box. And Ben Tolliver's email page came up on the screen! I scanned his Inbox and found what I was looking for! *10/13/2004, 1:26 a.m.* From Ben Tolliver to Ben Tolliver. Subject: "To Bulldog."

Bulldog. I can't keep running. I'm going to the police. If you want to stop me, meet me outside Harry's. Tonight, 10 pm. I'm ready to talk about a deal.

My heart raced. *Tonight!* Less than six hours from now, Ben was going to meet Bulldog! I read the "To" and "From" lines again. He had sent the email to himself! That didn't make sense.

Or did it? Ben knew exactly who would be monitoring his Hotmail. The same person who pulled up an email from Rachel Monday night just minutes after I'd let it slip that Ben's girlfriend might be contacting him that way.

The only computer guru I knew.

Chapter Thirty-one

I reread Ben's email with unbelieving eyes and a hammering heart. I checked my watch. Four fifteen. At ten, Ben would be meeting Bulldog at Harry's. A gigantic boulder of sadness settled onto my psyche, forcing me to admit I'd been clinging to a thread of hope that the killer would turn out to be someone other than Jack—like a drug dealer. But no drug dealer could monitor Ben's Hotmail.

Meet me outside Harry's, Ben had written. That would be Harry Nagorski, Ben's and Jessie's friend. Would Jack know who Harry was? Of course. He drove their carpool home after practice one day when Gordy didn't show.

I tried to call Underwood. Four rings, a click, then more rings. Finally a voice barked, "Detective Lewis."

With a sinking feeling, I identified myself and asked for Underwood.

"He's out right now. May I help you?"

"He's out? Is Detective Domagala in?"

"No, can I help you?"

I gathered my thoughts. "This is Anna Sebastian. I need to talk to someone who's familiar with the case of the missing teenager, Ben Tolliver."

"You got information?" I could almost hear the officer snap to attention.

I talked fast. "I found an email he sent. He's going to meet someone called Bulldog at ten o'clock tonight outside the Nagorskis' house, half a block from the Tollivers' trailer."

"Back up a minute." His voice had jumped an octave. "How'd you find this email?"

"Ben snuck into my house last night, and I just discovered that he used my computer."

There was a moment's silence. Then, "Hold on, let me see if I can get hold of Underwood."

After what seemed like at least ten minutes, Underwood's brisk voice came on the line. "Lewis says you found an email from Ben Tolliver."

"Yes." I read it to him. "He sent it to himself. At first, I thought he'd made a mistake, but then I realized he'd expect Jack Braxton to be monitoring his email."

"Braxton," he echoed. "Yeah." He drew the word out into two syllables. "Yeah, that makes sense. Who the hell is this Bulldog he's writing to?"

"Ben talked about Bulldog in the poem I found at Jack's house, remember? I think it's a nickname. It could be a nickname for Jack—he was a Georgia Bulldog. But whoever he is, I'm pretty sure Bulldog killed Jessie."

I waited for him to ask how I'd come to that conclusion, but he didn't. "Who's Harry?"

"Harry Nagorski, the Tollivers' neighbor. He lives half a block down from them in a gray house that backs up to Dalton Street Pond. It's the only place near the pond that's occupied."

I thought the silence on the other end of the line might swallow me up before Underwood responded. "Would your boyfriend know this Harry?"

Ignoring a white flash of rage, I tried to answer with dignity. "He's not my boyfriend, but yes, Jack knows him—and where he lives. Harry was on Ben's football team, and Jack drove both boys home from practice one day."

"OK. Good job. I'll double-check the email. If he sent it to himself, our guys should have it by now."

"You'll case out the Nagorskis' place?"

"You bet." After a moment he added, "And you will stay home tonight, right?"

"Of course." How stupid did he think I was? I pictured the Nagorskis' house and the pond behind it where Jessie had been murdered. Did Underwood really think I would venture into that scene? "Don't worry, the only place I'm going tonight is over to the nursing home to visit my mother."

Chapter Thirty-two

My mother's vacant eyes drifted toward my face as I tucked a pillow behind her back and moved her tray closer. "Yumm, noodles," I said with forced enthusiasm. "Dinner looks good tonight, Mom."

As I gathered a small spoonful and coaxed it into my mother's mouth, her nurse Reba bustled in. "Antibiotics are starting to work," she told me as she watched my mother chew the tiny bite a long time and finally swallow it.

"Looks like it," I said, stabbing a green bean with a fork. "How are things going for you? Is it still a zoo around here?"

Reba rolled her eyes. "Oh, yeah! Now there's talk about missing prescription drugs over at Sunset Days next door. Still none here I know of, but I feel like I got the Gestapo looking over my shoulder every minute." She hurried on her way. I stayed until Mom started spitting food down her chin.

When I got home, the clock was striking the half hour—6:30. I paced the small circle from my kitchen to the living room to the dining area, back to the kitchen. With every step, I thought about Ben's meeting with Bulldog. Had Underwood and his entourage already stationed themselves around the Nagorski home to watch and wait? I pictured the officers crouched in the untrimmed bushes of the neighboring vacant houses. Would they intercept Ben? Would they catch Jack?

When my legs began to grumble about my pacing, I sat down at the kitchen table and found myself staring at the Tolliver file, still lying there where I'd left it. Suddenly curious, I turned to Ben's poems. I practically knew them by heart, but to refresh my memory, I reread the first one, *The Dark,* searching for any reference to Ben's dead brother, Leon. The beginning of the poem told of bad things happening at night that no one was allowed to talk about. Going to bed hungry, dreaming of food, and waking to the nightmare of empty cupboards. There was the strange line about a serpent slithering over stones. And howling dogs. None of this seemed to relate to Leon. But the last stanza echoed Mama's words about the grandson she had lost. *The lamb is abandoned, the angel forsaken.*

Strange. These powerful images felt like the climax of the whole poem, yet nothing else in it seemed to refer to Leon. Was I missing something?

My gaze drifted back to the most puzzling line: *The serpent shows its fangs and slithers over the stones.* Serpent was a biblical word, for sure. Even I knew the story of Adam and Eve. The *Concordance to the Bible* Kate had loaned me still lay on the kitchen counter where I'd dropped it last night. Deciding that a bit of biblical research could help me pass the time while I waited for news from the police, I dragged it to the table and opened it to the S's.

The word *serpent* yielded half a column of references. There was the serpent who tempted Eve. And the rod of Moses, turned into a serpent. Scanning the list, I stopped at Psalm 58:4. *The wicked have venom like the venom of a serpent.* Ben was writing about wicked people, wasn't he? I tried to picture a young boy connecting bad people with a verse from the Psalms. I couldn't.

I continued down the page. My heart skipped a beat when I came to Proverbs 30:19—*the way of a serpent on a rock.* Ben's poem mentioned a serpent slithering over stones! Locating the verse in the Bible, I discovered it told of things *too wonderful for me—the way of an eagle in the sky, the way of a serpent on a rock.* Things too wonderful? A snake showing its fangs and slithering away? Hardly. I let my forehead drop down onto the book. Nothing hung together.

The clock chimed seven. Forcing myself to concentrate, I turned back to the list of references in the concordance. *Serpent* appeared in Isaiah, Jeremiah, and Amos, but none of these texts seemed likely. Running my finger down the page to the New Testament references, I stopped at Matthew 7:10.—*or if he ask a fish, will give him a serpent?* In his poem, Ben dreamed about tuna fish. And the serpent appeared in the next stanza. Could there possibly be a connection? Without much optimism, I looked up the verse in the Bible.

The full sentence in the seventh chapter of Matthew began at verse nine. *What man of you, if his son asks him for bread, will give him a stone? Or if he asks for a fish, will give him a serpent?* Bread and stone! Fish and serpent! Reading a little further, I saw that Jesus was comparing God's care to the kindness of a human father. *If you then, who are evil, know how to give good gifts to your children, how much more will your Father who is in heaven give good things to those who ask him!* No human father would give his son a stone if he asked for bread—or a serpent if he asked for fish. So said Jesus. But not in Ben's poem!

With racing heart, I read Ben's lines. *Dreams in dark bedrooms—white bread and tuna. Reach out with hope. Wake to the nightmare. The serpent shows its fangs and slithers over the stones.* When Ben asked his father for white bread and tuna, he got serpent and stone!

Could that possibly be Ben's meaning? Could these obscure symbols refer to Ben's father?

As I stared at the words, I pictured Mama quoting these verses to Gordy, perhaps to criticize the way he handled his sons. And young Ben taking it all in. For a moment I was too shocked to think. Then a rush of possibilities surged through my mind like a damn breaking. If serpent and stone, bread and fish were about Gordy Tolliver, what about other symbols in Ben's poems?

Shaken, I picked up *Forsaken Angel,* the poem I'd found under the mattress in Jack's guest room. There was the forsaken angel who fell into fire and water. Now I knew that referred to Leon. Then there were the dogs who swarmed the heavenly city—bad people who should have been locked out. The last stanza caught my eye. *Peace is a phantom; only death is real. Three against two; two against three. And one against all.* Death was all too real; Ben had lost two brothers. And of course he felt alone against the world. But what was the point of *three against two?* If the *two* were Ben and Jessie, who were the three? And why this particular wording? Did Ben pull it out of thin air? Or did it come from the Bible like the "bread," the "serpent," the "angel who fell into fire and water," and the "dogs" who break down the "gates of the city"?

Back to the concordance. I looked up *three,* and two minutes later, I had the quote! Luke 12:51-52! I read the passage in horrified amazement. How could a loving grandmother read stuff like this to a child?   I pictured Mama reciting Bible passages to her young grandson when he misbehaved instead of giving him a Time Out. First, she'd quote a string of end-of-the-world scenarios from *Revelation* to put the fear of God into him. Then she'd top it off with this dire passage from Luke.

> *Do you think that I have come to bring peace on the earth? No, I tell you, but rather division. For henceforth in one house there will be five divided, three against two and two against three; they will be divided: father against son and son against father.*

In one house, there will be five divided. Tiffany, Gordy, Ben, Jessie. Leon. *Three against two, two against three.* The exact words of Ben's poem. Parents against children. *Father against son.*

I felt my head begin to pound. Gordy Tolliver against his son? Which son?

Ever since I had learned about Leon, I'd wondered why Ben wrote a poem about his youngest brother's death right after his other brother was murdered. It didn't make sense unless— . Unless the two deaths were connected!

Father against son and son against father.

Gordy had been home alone with the children when little Leon had his fatal convulsion. Was there an autopsy? If Gordy had stopped the boy's breathing with his hand or a pillow over his face during a seizure, would an autopsy even have shown that? Could Gordon Tolliver have murdered his retarded, mute, epileptic son? Could Ben have seen him do it?

And what about Jessie's death? Gordy knew Jessie was home that day. The school always contacted him when his son was absent—Tiffany told me that. Was this call from the school the proverbial straw that broke the last shred of Gordy's patience with his brain-damaged son? Did he roar home with the intention of giving Jessie a good thrashing—then totally lose his cool?

No! I couldn't believe it! Anyway, Gordy had a solid alibi. Underwood said he'd been at work the whole day, and other staff had confirmed his presence.

Other staff? What other staff? Could someone have lied to protect Gordy? Why would anyone do that? My mind drifted back to my conversation with my mother's nurse at Hibiscus Villa earlier this evening. Extra security was making her life a zoo, she'd said. Prescription drugs were disappearing from Sunset Days Care Center, next door. Where Gordy worked! Prescription medications like Oxycontin, the pills the police found in an unmarked bottle the day Tiffany died?

Gordy couldn't have known that Ben came home from school with a headache the same day Jessie played hooky. Did Ben see what happened? Did Gordy somehow discover that Ben had witnessed the whole thing? Is that why Ben ran away? Was it Gordy who stationed himself outside Ben's hideout—and took a shot at me?

It was all pure speculation. Yet if Bulldog was Gordy's nickname, Tiffany would surely have recognized it when I showed her Ben's poetry. Probably she would also have picked up the title of Ben's poem *Forsaken Angel* as a reference to Leon. Is that what she wanted to tell me when she asked me to meet her? And what about the email Ben sent from my computer? Gordy could easily have known how to monitor his son's Hotmail account. Was Gordy

Tolliver the one Ben planned to meet outside Harry Nagorski's house tonight?

Stop it, Anna! Stop it, stop it, stop it! You don't have a shred of proof. If Bulldog is Gordy, the police will catch him tonight. Stay out of it. Don't mess up their work like you did the last time.

Even as I lectured myself, a deep unease niggled at my mind. Why? Was it about something in the poems? If so, I couldn't identify it. Was it about Ben's email? *Meet me outside Harry's,* Ben had said.

Harry's! That's what had been bothering me! The Nagorskis' house seemed a dangerous place to meet. Why would Ben pick a spot right in his own neighborhood? Wouldn't the police be keeping constant surveillance on the whole block in case the runaway returned to his trailer? Wouldn't Ben know that? Why not meet somewhere safer?

What if "Harry's" wasn't Harry Nagorski's house? What if Ben's email meant a different Harry's?

I began to pace. Kitchen, dining room, living room, entrance hall, back to the kitchen. *Harry's, Harry's, Harry's.* I repeated the name in time to my marching feet. Why meet in a neighborhood where anyone who happened to see them might report them as prowlers? Why not meet somewhere less conspicuous, a place where people come and go without attracting attention, like a convenience store or a restaurant?

A restaurant! I had a sudden flash of memory.

Racing back to the kitchen, I grabbed the Tolliver case file. My fingers trembled so uncontrollably I could hardly find the page I wanted. Then miraculously, the information was right in front of my eyeballs. At the time Gordon and Tiffany Tolliver petitioned the court for custody of their sons, Gordon was employed in the kitchen at Harpoon Harry's, the popular bar and restaurant at the end of the pier in the outdoor mall, Fishermen's Village. He'd quit—or been fired— a few months later and took a janitor's job at Sunset Days Care Center.

Meet me outside Harry's. What if Ben's email didn't mean Harry Nagorski's? What if it meant Harpoon Harry's! A lot of stores in the outdoor mall were still closed, but I remembered reading that Harpoon Harry's had just reopened.

I grabbed my phone and dialed 911. No point calling Underwood's office; he and his team would be at the Nagorskis' house, waiting for two people who might never show up.

I identified myself to the female voice who answered. "Can you put me in touch with Detective Underwood? It's important."

"I can get a message to him."

I started to argue, then decided not to waste precious minutes. "Tell him this," I said. "Tell him I don't think Ben Tolliver will show up at Harry Nagorski's house; I think he's going to Harpoon Harry's at Fishermen's Village. Do you have that?" An affirmative grunt. "And tell him I don't think Ben is meeting Jack Braxton; I think he's meeting his father, Gordon Tolliver."

Chapter Thirty-three

At half past eight, Underwood called with news. "We got your boyfriend. He pulled up in a silver Camry a few houses down from Nagorskis' place."

I sank down onto the high stool at my kitchen counter. So it was Jack after all. "Did you catch Ben?"

"Not yet, but we will. What's this about Gordon Tolliver?"

"I figured out some of the symbolism in the poem Ben wrote after Jessie's death. It made me suspect that Gordy was Bulldog—you know, the bad guy in the poem?"

"Guess you were wrong. Those poems are mostly gibberish."

"They're not gibberish, but hard to understand."

"What's that?"

I started to repeat myself, but Underwood cut me off with a hasty "Gotta go," and I realized he hadn't been talking to me. I stared at the dial tone for a moment before I gathered enough presence of mind to hang up.

As my grand theory fizzled, I let my head fall into my hands. I probably shouldn't have been surprised. All the evidence pointed toward Jack except my interpretation of Ben's poems. A cold fury took hold of me. How dare Underwood call Jack my boyfriend! Just thinking about Jack made my skin crawl. I hated him for taking me in with his nice guy act. And I hated myself for buying into it. Well, I never did have good judgment about men! If I did, I never would have married Drew. Anyway, the police had Jack in custody, and they'd soon have Ben. I'd read too much into the poems, that's all. Maybe they really were gibberish, like Underwood said.

I raised my head just enough to rest my chin in my hand like The Thinker. Only I wasn't thinking. My brain was a vacuum. Drained. Awhile later—maybe ten minutes or maybe only two or three—I became aware of the pulsing of a repeated question somewhere in the blankness of my mind.

What if I wasn't wrong?

Why was Underwood so sure Ben wouldn't go to Harpoon Harry's? Because Jack showed up at the Nagorskis' place, that's why. Still, Jack and Gordy could both have monitored Ben's email. Jack had obviously assumed, as I did at first, that "Harry's" meant the Nagorskis' house. Would Gordy? What if he and Ben turned up at Harpoon Harry's at ten o'clock—an hour and a half from now?

Underwood thought he had his man, so he discounted my message. And he probably wouldn't dispatch anyone to Fishermen's Village. How I wished I could make myself invisible and go to Harpoon Harry's to see if Ben or Gordy showed up.

The silly thought triggered an idea. If I did it right, I might be able to come close to making myself invisible. Who would notice an innocuous older woman sitting at a table in a popular bar and restaurant? My closet still held half a rack of Mom's clothes. Could I make myself unrecognizable? Maybe. Did I have the nerve? Possibly. If not, could I sit quietly at home, meekly following Underwood's instructions, while Ben either got killed or became a murderer himself?

No way!

I chose Mother's silky beige blouse—a color that gave my skin a greenish cast. Perfect. Added a matching floozy sweater and a pair of my own dressy tan slacks. To my delight, I found a gray wig left over from the days when Mom's mind had been sharp enough to worry about her thinning hair. I removed the prescription lenses from a pair of her owlish glasses and topped off the outfit with thick mascara and fire-engine lipstick. A pocketbook adorned with pink flamingos completed my disguise. Looking in the mirror, I decided I looked forty years older.

As I backed out of my driveway, the thought occurred to me that I should let someone know where I was going just in case something went wrong. I braked and punched Kate's number into my cell phone. Got her answering machine. "Kate, it's Anna," I said after the tone. "I'm on a mission. It's too complicated to explain in this message, but the short version is that I intercepted an email from Ben that says he plans to meet Bulldog at Harry's at ten o'clock tonight. I think he means Harpoon Harry's. Underwood doesn't agree—so I'm going over to Fishermen's Village to see if Ben turns up. I'm wearing my mother's clothes, so I don't think he'll notice me. I won't do anything rash. If I catch sight of Ben, I'll get out of there fast and call 911. I'll call you when I get home. I just wanted someone to know where I'm going."

Twenty minutes later, I pulled into the Fisherman's Village parking lot. It was sparsely filled; in fact, the whole place still resembled a war zone. The sign dangled at half mast and temporary floodlights replaced the original light poles, many of which bent over at the waist like hunchbacks. In my rented Chevy, I crept up and down the sparse rows of cars, searching for Gordy's black pickup and my stolen white Ford Focus, which I assumed Ben would still be using for wheels. I inspected every vehicle for an extra antenna that might indicate an unmarked police car. Signs of a solid police presence would mean Underwood had taken my hunch about Harpoon Harry's seriously, and I could turn around and bolt for home. To my dismay, I found nothing. Not my Focus, not Gordy's truck, not a sign of police.

I was scared. Not just nervous, not just anxious. I was gut-curdling, muscle-twitching, knee-knocking scared. I had to clench my jaw to keep my teeth from chattering.

Checking my image in the visor mirror, I didn't recognize the face that stared back at me. Good. I should be able to walk through the mall incognito and saunter casually to the far end and into Harpoon Harry's. Ben's email said "outside Harry's." By "outside," I was pretty sure he meant the narrow dock along the side of the restaurant where boaters tied up during the daytime. The dock should be lighted, so I'd be able to gain a decent view from one of the tables that overlooked it. I'd nurse a beer and keep watch. If Ben or Gordy really did appear, I could slip into the ladies' room and call 911 on my cell phone.

Gathering my courage, I got out of my car and entered the mall, trying for nonchalance. The promenade was nearly deserted except for an older couple who smiled at me as they passed. Some of the shops were boarded up, and most of the others were closed for the night, but I hoped a variety store and a coffee shop would still be open, along with Harpoon Harry's. The temperature had dropped at least ten degrees since the sun set, and the covered walkway down the center of the open-air mall funneled the wind. Pulling Mother's lacy sweater to my chin, I wished for my traditional sweatshirt. I was glad I'd made the decision to wear my own shoes.

Just beyond the first crosswalk that led out toward the yacht basin, I stopped to gaze at a temporary metal structure that looked something like a giant Tinker Toy. Following its framework upward with my eyes, I saw that it held up long steel beams that seemed to be supporting the ceiling and the second story. The shops and restaurants along the promenade at Fisherman's Village had come out of the hurricane bruised and battered yet still largely intact. But in the second story condos, 145-mile-an-hour sustained winds had ravaged the roof and shattered plate glass windows, doing over three million dollars worth of damage. Obviously, the popular timeshares that overlooked both sides of the promenade would be closed for repair and renovation for some time. Gazing down the length of the mall, I realized that more temporary metal support structures had been placed at regular intervals as far as I could see, casting eerie shadows in the glow from the makeshift light fixtures. The once festive tourist destination had turned into a metal jungle.

A trio of giggling teens passed by, barely giving me a second glance. As I passed the darkened shops, I peered into every alcove, hoping to see a burly figure who looked like a cop on duty. No such luck. Two chattering couples dawdled toward me, the women peering in windows of the closed shops and letting out high shrieks of laughter. They didn't look like police.

The desolation gave me the creeps. I crossed another open driveway. Beyond it, a blocked stairway led to the timeshares, and yet another metal support structure stretched upward. Halfway past it, I screeched to a stop. Wedged into the V of its crosspiece, just above my eye level, was a child's stuffed toy. A dog, all black except for one white ear. One button eye was missing, and its head drooped a bit to the left.

Floyd!

Involuntarily, my eyes traveled to the open-air walkway that ran along the front of the second story condos. Directly above me, a white paint cloth that hung over the railing rippled slightly. I fumbled in Mom's flamingo pocketbook for my cell phone. Too late! Before I could get my hands on it, a figure flew through the barricade at the bottom of the stairs, sending the purse flying and knocking me flat. Blinding pain flashed a rainbow in my head when I landed.

Chapter Thirty-four

What was that sound I was hearing?. Water. Waves on the shore. Then a deeper noise. The waves were getting closer. No, that wasn't right. The low sound was more like a grunt! Someone in pain. Or working hard. Breathing! That's what I was hearing. Not waves, breathing! Someone breathing hard. I was moving. Someone was carrying me. The breathing, grunting person was carrying me.

I ordered my eyes to open, but they refused. Still, my memory was coming back. Fishermen's Village. The metal scaffold beside the stairs. Floyd. The creature that lunged at me before I could grab my cell phone. That's who was carrying me. The creature was carrying me up the stairs.

The breathing had a wheeze in it now. He was struggling. Or crying?

Finally my eyes obeyed my command and I caught a glimpse of a black sweatshirt, a neck and a chin. A scrawny neck with a prominent Adams apple. A smooth chin. Young.

Ben. It had to be Ben.

I snapped my eyes shut. I hadn't seen his face, so he couldn't know I was conscious. *Keep it that way. Act like dead weight.* Who was I kidding? I *was* dead weight.

I felt myself being lowered, then falling like a corpse. It took every ounce of will power to keep from flinching when my shoulder hit the floor, but the pain wasn't as bad as I expected. He probably hadn't dropped me more than a foot, and the flooring felt like wood.

The wheezing continued. "Wake up, Anna." His voice cracked. He smelled of sweat and poor hygiene. Feeling his hot breath on my ear lobes, I realized my wig was gone. It must have cushioned the blow when my head hit the concrete on the promenade below. When had it fallen off? Was it now lying in front of a darkened dress shop where a passer-by might notice it? I concentrated on making like a mummy.

The telltale whisk of denim against denim told me Ben was moving away, and I risked a peek. Mimicking the first flutter of a person returning to consciousness, I flicked my eyelids. In that split second, I took in a narrow walkway that faded from gray into blackness, punctuated by occasional triangles of light. On my right was a waist-high railing, and on my left a wall lined with doors. We were on the upper level of Fishermen's Village in front of the storm-damaged condos that overlooked the shops below. A workers' drop cloth hanging over the railing protected us from the view of people passing by on the promenade. I couldn't see Ben. He must be behind me. Yes, I could hear him huffing. Did I dare risk turning my head?

Cautiously, I tilted my chin a few degrees, expecting him to pounce any minute. When he didn't, I chanced another quick blink. Reflected light shone through the small opening he had made in the drop cloth, illuminating his profile as he sat on the walkway. His pistol rested on his bent knees, poised to swing in either direction. He had baited his trap with his stuffed dog, and now like a hunter laying for his prey, he watched the promenade below.

So I'd been right. Bulldog had to be Gordy Tolliver. No one else would recognize the stuffed dog. Ben had assumed Gordy was monitoring his email and would receive his invitation to meet. And he knew the familiar toy would stop his dad in his tracks as he came by on his way to Harpoon Harry's. In that brief moment of surprise, he would present a perfect target!

Would Ben really kill him? I stole another glance at his face. I fully believed he would do it.

Could I possibly talk him out of it? I had to try. But if I couldn't, then what? Going for his gun was out of the question. Right now, even the thought of sitting up seemed a daunting challenge. I was in no shape for a physical contest with a fifteen-year-old boy. Could I possibly get away and call for help? We weren't far from the stairs. If I could make it even half way down before he came after me, I might have a chance. I didn't think he'd shoot me in the back. Even if he tried, he was a novice with a gun, and I'd be a moving target. There were people in the promenade below—and at Harpoon Harry's. Not many, but perhaps enough. I might even find my purse—with my cell phone in it—where Ben had knocked it out of my hand.

Distract him. That was my best hope.

With a sudden jerk of his head, he caught me staring at him and swung the gun toward me. "Why couldn't you keep your nose out of this, Anna?" he asked disgustedly. "How'd you find me anyway?"

"I read the email you sent from my computer."

The gun shook visibly, and he steadied it with both hands. "You shouldn't have come."

"Don't do this, Ben," I pleaded. "I'm on your side." I saw his eyes dart to the promenade then back to me. "And I know about your father."

He recoiled as if I had struck him.

Chapter Thirty-five

Male and female voices drifted up from the promenade below, but Ben paid no attention. "What do you mean, 'you know about my father'?"

OK, here goes. "I know he killed your brothers—both of them," I said.

Blinking rapidly, he croaked, "What are you talking about?"

I rolled over on my side to face him. "I tracked down a neighbor who knew your grandmother. Mama. She told me about Leon. He didn't die from an epileptic seizure, did he?"

Like an animal ready to spring, Ben rose to a half crouch, keeping the gun trained on my chest. As I propped my head on an elbow, I saw the pistol twitch in his hand. "How did he do it, Ben?" I pressed. "Did he hold a pillow over your brother's face?"

"How can you know that?" he whispered.

Moving very, very slowly so as not to alarm him, I struggled to a sitting position. "I read it in your poems."

For one fleeting second he looked straight at me, his eyes wide as silver dollars. "My poems?"

"'Forsaken angel, guilty of nothing, punished forever. Three against two, two against three. Father against son; son against father.' And 'Bulldog.' That's your dad's nickname, isn't it?"

Glancing out at the promenade, he snorted. "My mother called him that to tease him because his bottom jaw sticks out." His gaze shifted back to the promenade, and I edged an inch to my right, toward the stairs. Instantly, he swung his head toward me.

Hoping to keep him too distracted to notice that I'd moved, I pushed on. "You saw him kill Leon."

We stared into the shadows of each other's faces, unspoken horror rising like a specter between us. Then slowly, he sat back down on the wooden walkway, resting the pistol on one knee. With an almost imperceptible nod, he said, "He hated having a kid who wasn't normal."

"My God, Ben! You never told anyone?"

He shook his head. I waited for him to make some kind of explanation. When he didn't, I prodded. "Why didn't you?"

He lowered his head. "I don't know," he murmured.

I decided not to press the issue. I had too many other questions. "And when he came back last year, why did you agree to live with him?"

He snuck another look down the promenade, but his face wasn't turned long enough for me to risk a move. "Jessie wanted to live with his 'real' mom and dad, and I couldn't talk him out of it." His right cheek twitched.

"So you moved with him." As he had done so many times before. "To protect him."

He closed his eyes for a second, and I slipped sideways two inches before he jerked them open warily.

I talked fast to keep him distracted. "But you couldn't protect him. Gordy killed Jessie too, didn't he? He came home from the nursing home on a break and found your brother out playing on that dock he and Harry built, didn't he? Struck him with a short beam of aluminum from someone's pool cage. Didn't he?"

Ben swayed toward the railing. In the light from below, his eyes glowed like a trapped animal's. "I'm going to kill him," he said between clenched teeth. "Don't think you can stop me, Anna." To drive home his point, he raised his gun with both hands until I found myself staring straight down its barrel.

Trying not to look at it, I threw another question at him. "Why did he do it, Ben? Why did he kill Jessie?"

Although his head was turned toward me, he didn't meet my gaze, and he blinked at least ten times. "Jessie found out about Leon."

"Only now—after all these years? How?"

He made another quick check of the scene below, and I moved another inch. "It's a long story," he said. I watched his chest rise and fall and felt my own breathing keep rhythm with it. When he was satisfied that no one was coming, he said, "Jessie and my father had a big, stupid fight. It was over nothing, really, but you know my brother's temper. He landed his fist in my dad's gut, and I was afraid my dad would hurt him real bad, so I hauled Jessie off him. My father stomped away, but then Jessie started pounding on me. Finally I got so mad I just lost it. I yelled, 'He was gonna kill you!' Jessie still kept slugging—didn't realize I meant it, so I flattened him. I pinned his shoulders to the floor and told him, 'He was gonna kill you like he killed Leon.' I didn't mean to say it, and I didn't think I said it very loud, but I glanced over to the door and saw my father staring at me."

"Oh, Ben," I said softly. "Oh Ben, oh Ben, oh Ben." He turned away, made a show of scanning the promenade.

I was too stunned to move. "And the next day, you came home with a headache from school and your dad didn't know you were there. Where were you when he killed Jessie?"

He was quiet so long, I thought I'd pushed him too hard. But finally he murmured, "Out behind Nagorskis' house." Dumbstruck, I waited for what seemed forever before he added, "Mom dropped me off at the corner, and I knew my brother would be playing over there. That's what he always did when he cut school. I was just going to holler to him so he'd know I was home."

For a brief second, he leaned into the rail to get a longer view. While he focused on the promenade, I moved again.

His head jerked toward me, and I thought he'd sensed my movement, but then he continued. "I saw him charge through the bushes onto the dock with something in his hand. He was still wearing scrubs from work. He swung, and Jessie fell backward into the pond. Before I could move, my dad looked over and saw me."

"And you ran."

"He came after me in his truck, but I climbed into the bed of an open pickup a block away. I watched his old green Ford crawl up the street toward me, and I thought for sure he'd find me, but pretty soon he drove off."

"He had to get back to work before people started asking where he was."

"I guess."

"What did you do then?

"I slipped into the Nagorskis' house. No one was home, but I know where they keep a key. I called . . . someone I knew. I said I was running away from home and I needed help. So he came and picked me up."

My heart turned a somersault inside my chest. "Coach Jack."

"So?" His voice took on its old defiant edge, and he scanned the promenade.

"Did you tell him what happened?"

He shook his head. "He asked, but I didn't want to talk about it."

"And he just let you stay there? He didn't . . . do anything?"

"Yeah, he did. He kept trying to talk me into letting him take me to the police. He said he'd pay for a lawyer, but I wasn't going to no cops. At first he didn't bug me about it, but after a couple days, I started to get the feeling he was going to call them even if I said no. Then Rachel sent me an email—the coach let me play games on his computer. She warned me that you'd been asking questions about Coach Jack. So I split."

"Why didn't you tell Jack what you saw?"

"I don't know. I just couldn't." He sat motionless for a long time. "It was all my fault, Anna," he said finally.

How could that be? "You couldn't tell him your dad killed Jessie because it was all your fault?"

He gave the slightest nod, not looking at me but keeping me within his peripheral vision.

"What was your fault, Ben?"

He stared at his revolver, steadying it against his knee.

Finally I repeated my question. "What was your fault?"

"Leon," he whispered.

"Leon?" I couldn't believe I'd heard him right. "Your dad didn't hold a pillow over his face?"

"Yeah, he did, but first—" He closed his eyes for a moment, then hastily glanced down at the promenade. When he turned back to me, he murmured, "I guess I can tell you about it. It doesn't matter anyway." He was talking to his knees. "Before all that happened—" He screwed up his face until I thought he might burst into tears. "Before Leon had the seizure, I . . . shook him."

For what seemed an eternity he was silent. Then his words poured out like lava. "He kept whining—he couldn't talk, you know—and he kept holding his hands up to me giving me that half cry, half whine he did all the time, and I told him to be quiet but he wouldn't, so finally I shook him, yelling 'Shut up, shut up, shut up!'" Ben lowered his head. "I shook him," he repeated softly.

When I didn't say anything, he went on. "We were in our bedroom—me and Jessie and Leon all had the same room. My dad came to see what the yelling was about and saw me shaking Leon. And then—" He broke off.

"And then?"

"Then Leon had a seizure. My dad said, 'Now see what you've gone and done. You made him have a spell.' Leon was writhing on the floor, but my dad wasn't looking at him. He just kept glaring at me. He said, 'You hate having a brother who's not normal, don't you?' At first I didn't say anything, but he kept asking me that over and over till finally I said, 'Yeah, I do.' He said, 'You hate it when he has seizures, don't you?' I said, 'yeah.' He said, 'Shall I make it stop?' I said, 'Can you do that?' And he said, 'Sure, do you want me to?' And I said, 'yeah.' That's when my dad put a pillow over his face. And after awhile—after a really long time—my brother's body stopped thrashing."

Ben looked out toward the promenade, but I doubted that he saw anything except the scene that replayed in his mind. As for me, I was way too shaken to think about making another move toward the stairs.

Turning back toward me, Ben continued his painful story. Now that he had started talking, it seemed he couldn't stop. "After Leon got quiet, my dad said, 'We can't tell anyone about this, Buddy. We're in it together, you and me. I only did what you told me to do. You'll be in bad trouble if anyone finds out. But no one needs to. Ever. OK?'"

Ben swiped his cheeks with his hand. "And I never told anyone. Till Jessie and my dad had that big fight, and I ended up screaming the truth at him. If I'd kept my mouth shut like I promised, my dad wouldn't have heard me, and Jessie wouldn't have known about it, and he'd still be alive." Tears were streaming down his cheeks now, but he kept choking out words. "And I never tried to save him. I didn't call 911—or even go over to the dock to pull him out of the water to see if he was still alive." He wiped his cheeks and nose on the sleeve of his T-shirt. "I was too chicken."

I wanted to put my arms around him, but instead I said very firmly, "Leon's death is not your fault, Ben. When you told your dad you wanted the seizures to stop, you didn't know he meant to kill him, did you?"

"No." The words stretched long like he wasn't sure he meant it. He glanced at me, then quickly looked away. "But deep down, Anna, I wasn't really sorry he was gone."

"That's not the same as killing him. You would never have done that. Your father killed Leon, and then he blamed you to keep you from telling anyone about it. It was not your fault. And Jessie's death wasn't either. You told Jessie about Leon because you were trying to protect him. And of course you didn't go over to the dock after your dad struck him. You were running away from a man who had already killed your brothers and who was trying to kill you. Even if you had gone back, you couldn't have saved Jessie's life. He was dead before he hit the water." To my surprise, Ben met my gaze for a long moment, and I felt a surge of hope. "None of this was your fault, Ben. No one can possibly blame you. Please let me call the police. I'll tell them you witnessed Jessie's murder."

"The police have screwed up my life enough already, thank you," he scoffed, sliding his protective shell firmly back into place. He shifted his position to take his weapon in both hands, pointing it toward the trap he had set for his father on the promenade below.

"No!" I pleaded. "It'll be different this time. The police will arrest your father. You don't have to kill him. He'll go to jail for life. Don't make yourself a murderer, Ben. Please. Let the police handle it."

"The police!" He fairly spat the words. "They'll be so busy arresting me, they'll let my father get away. And that can't happen." He glanced at me as he spoke through gritted teach. "He's got Rachel."

"What?"

"I heard about her on your car radio. Rachel wouldn't run away. I know my father's got her. He thinks he can use her to get to me." His hands held his weapon in a death grip as he sighted on his target below.

"Listen to me, Ben. I know the detectives who are working this case. They're rational human beings. If you let me go, I'll contact them and tell them the whole story. I can make them believe me. They'll arrest your father, and if he has Rachel, they'll find her."

He looked my way just long enough to make sure I hadn't moved. "You mean well, Anna, but you don't know anything about my world. You think the police are rational human beings." His voice dripped with scorn.

"I know terrible things have happened to you, Ben, but . . ."

"Drop it, Anna," he snapped. "There's no way out of this for me."

I let out a long sigh of disappointment. For a few minutes, I'd thought I had a real chance of gaining his trust, but now I realized

Ben couldn't trust anyone. He'd been betrayed too many times. The next time he gazed down the promenade, I risked a longer sideways slide.

Big mistake! Ben caught the motion, whipped around, and sprang. Dodging, I leaped to my feet and swung at him. The gun clattered onto the walkway, and I dove for it. Touched it. Felt it slide from my fingers. Watched it skid to a stop under a fold of the drop cloth as Ben grabbed my right arm. I tried to strike with my left, but he overpowered me. For a skinny kid, he was amazingly strong. He wrestled me across the narrow walkway and pinned both my arms above my head against one of the condo doors.

We panted into each other's faces. "There's no way out of this for me, Anna," Ben repeated. "I have to kill him. He. Is. Going. To. Die."

The voice—deep and familiar—came out of the darkness somewhere to my right. "I don't think so."

Ben and I turned as one to see a ghost-like and shivering Rachel York stumble up the steps. Close behind and jabbing a pistol into her back, was Gordy Tolliver.

"Hello Son," he said with his genial bulldog smile. "I knew you'd come to me once you figured out I had your girl." He gave his head a quick jerk toward me. "Just don't nobody move. No one needs to get hurt."

Chapter Thirty-six

In the illumination from below, Gordy's toothy grin glowed eerily while shadows seemed to elongate the top of his head. Rachel stumbled as he pressed his gun into her back, and he steadied her with his left hand. She was white in the dim light, and her once-spiked black hair straggled down to her eyebrows. The sleeves of her jacket hung loose, making me suspect her hands were tied behind her back. Her eyes glistened wide and vacant above her sharp cheek bones. There was something different about those eyes. Drugs, I bet.

"Rachel!" Ben cried. Letting go of me, he whirled around to face his father. "What have you done to her?"

"Don't move, Son," Gordy said softly, polite as always. "Don't move if you want her to keep her pretty head."

Ben froze.

As casually as if he were asking a simple favor, Gordy said, "Just do what I tell you. We got a cozy little party here, and if you're smart, we'll all come out OK. Just step away from the door, both of you, with your hands over your heads. Good. Now turn around and face the wall. Keep your hands up."

I obeyed. Fear was rapidly replacing the numbness of shock, and my teeth chattered. I sensed motion on my right, then heard a click followed by the creak of a swinging door. From somewhere behind me, Gordy spoke in a low voice. "Now slide along the wall to your right. Walk through the open door, and don't try to be heroes."

We didn't. A few moments later, we found ourselves inside one of the second-story condos. Its living room was partially illuminated by the soft glow from the walkway. A sliding glass door that probably led to an outer balcony had been boarded from the outside, but not before the hurricane had done its damage. Narrow slits of light—moonlight or an outdoor floodlight—filtered in around its edges, revealing a huge "X" someone had duct-taped fruitlessly across the glass to try to protect it from Charley's ferocious winds. A jagged reflection revealed a gaping hole, and shattered fragments clung to the "X" in hunks. The now useless roll of duct tape lay on the floor beneath the slider. Even though the place had been gutted of furniture, it still reeked of mildew.

"Backs against the wall." Gordy spoke softly, almost gently, but his tone—and the pistol in his hand—commanded our instant compliance. As I stumbled to obey, I felt something crunch under my feet against the bare floor. Fragments of glass from the shattered slider, most likely.

Dragging Rachel along with his arm around her throat, Gordy frisked me and Ben. Then he marched her over to the sliding door. "All right, Darling," he told the sniffling girl, "I'm going to untie your wrists. Then I want you to pick up that role of duct tape off the floor."

Turning to Ben, he said, "OK, Son, face the wall and lie on your stomach with your hands behind your back." Gordy spoke in the same tone he might use to say, "Eat your breakfast." A moment later, however, he dropped his nice guy act. "Now, Bud—if you care about your girlfriend's life." I heard Ben's ragged breathing as he left my side.

Across the small living room from where I stood, Ben dropped down to the floor. "Tape him up, Honey," Gordy instructed Rachel, "and don't make any noise. Hands first. That's right. Now his feet. Now his big, fat mouth." Inspecting her work, he said, "Good girl."

"OK, Ms. Guardian Ad Litem, you next." As I lowered myself down next to Ben, Gordy told Rachel, "Make it tight, Sweetheart. And don't take all night."

Rachel's touch was gentle, but she obeyed orders, pulling my bindings painfully tight. When the duct tape covered my mouth, I started to panic, but I lectured myself, *Calm down; breathe through your nose.* At last I felt blessed oxygen flow into my nostrils and lungs.

With a soft moan, Rachel took her place on the floor between me and the boarded slider. "Quiet now, honey," Gordy told her softly as he bound her. "No more moaning. I'm not going to say that again."

A light tinkle of laughter floated up from the promenade. Then a deeper voice said, "Evening, Officer." *Officer!* Had Underwood belatedly paid attention to my hunch? Or was it just a security guard working his routine beat at Fishermen's Village?

Gordy tiptoed to the door and eased it shut, plunging the room into darkness. The sudden blindness sent a fresh wave of panic through me, and I willed my heart to stop fluttering like a trapped bird. A policeman—at least one—was on the premises. There was hope.

Think!

The force of the hurricane must have scattered a lot of glass like the piece I'd crushed under my foot. If only I could get my hands on one, I might be able to saw through my duct-tape bindings. The darkness should help although now that my eyes were adjusting to it, I saw a feeble glow around the plywood that covered the sliding door, making shapes and outlines more clear. I stretched my bound wrists to the right as far as possible, but I couldn't touch the floor. To explore with my fingers for glass shards, I would have to roll over onto my side. How could I possibly do that without attracting Gordy's attention?

Rachel whimpered. Dropping the last vestige of his caring-and-concerned masquerade, Gordy sprinted to her and cracked his hand across her face. I wondered how I could ever have been so taken in by him. I thought about Rosemary Irving's comment: *Gordy was a charmer, could make you believe anything—first couple times anyway.* Yes, their former neighbor had his number. Rachel probably did too. She'd told me Ben hated living with his parents. I'd shrugged them both off. And now I was paying the price. Worse yet, Ben and Rachel were too.

Gordy gave Rachel's face another whack. "I told you 'no more moaning,'" he snarled. He was jumpy now. The presence of a policeman in the promenade below must have unnerved him. He stood over Rachel a long time. Then he inspected Ben and me. Apparently satisfied, he turned away. By raising my head and twisting from side to side, I was able to keep him in my sight as he crossed the room and sat down noiselessly on the floor. Now he was a mere black shape against the wall, dark on dark, but I thought I could make out his knees bent in front of him and the gun in his hand.

My mind whirled. If I couldn't see him clearly, then he couldn't see us any better. He'd pick up movement—I was pretty sure of that. But if I changed my position very gradually . . . . Like a slow-motion film, I let my right hip roll slightly toward the floor.

"OK, you cockroaches." Gordy's hushed voice sent a spasm of alarm through me, but I held my position. "You got one chance to live. You interested?"

As we bobbed our heads up and down, my index finger touched the floor.

Gordy didn't seem to see it. "Ben, your email said you wanted to negotiate. Here's the deal. In a little bit, when the coast is clear, we all walk out of here. Any of you utters a sound or tries to bolt, I shoot all three of you, starting with Rachel. If you make it to my truck alive, Ben, I drop you off somewhere. You turn yourself in to the police and confess you killed your brother Jessie." He paused while that sank in.

I touched something hard. As I slid my thumb over its edge, a sudden pain made me flinch. It was glass, all right—and sharp! My fingers explored its hard, flat surface. It was triangular shaped, maybe two inches wide at its base.

"And you, nosey Anna, maybe I let you go too, so—" He broke off, got up, and stood over me. Giving my right leg a vicious kick, he growled, "What do you think you're doing? Get back on your belly."

Stifling a moan of pain, I rolled back to my original position.

He stood over me for what seemed like several minutes before he continued. "Like I was saying, maybe I let you go too, so you can do your bleeding heart act for the judge, saying how it was an accident, how Ben didn't mean to kill him, all that crap. Maybe you get him sent to a looney farm instead of the poke. But I keep Pretty Rachel. Ben, you will convince the police you killed your brother. Anna, you'll make them buy it too. If you don't, Sweet Little Rachel here dies." He took a step toward her, and I saw clearly the outline of his outstretched arm, gun raised and pointed at the girl's prone form.

Dead silence followed this little speech. *A deal with the devil.* Would Ben agree to it? Would I?

Ben murmured something. I couldn't tell if it meant "Uh-huh" or Uh-uh," but Gordy seemed to take it as an affirmative. He snickered.

Then abruptly he stopped. "Shhh."

In the next instant, I understood why. A board creaked in the silence. Then another. Slow footsteps padded softly on the wooden walkway. Coming closer. Silhouetted against the soft glow around the plywood, Gordy pressed his gun to Rachel's head. "One sound and she's dead," he whispered.

It had to be the security guard—or the police. Who else would come up to this deserted place? I prayed whoever it was would spot Ben's gun where it had slid under the drop cloth. Was any part of it visible? I didn't know.

Our doorknob rattled. For what seemed forever, we held our collective breath. Finally the footsteps resumed. Our last chance to avoid the impossible choice that confronted us thumped slowly away.

Chapter Thirty-seven

As the footsteps faded, Gordy tiptoed to the doorway and pressed an ear to it. After listening for a time, he moved back into the center of the room. "OK," he said. "You did good. Keep behavin' yourselves and you won't get hurt."

Gordy stood over us for what seemed like at least ten minutes. Then finally he tiptoed around us and disappeared from view. Where had he gone? Had he actually left the living room? Soon the sound of water hitting water answered my question, reminding me of my own full bladder. *Forget that. Make use of these few precious minutes.*

Rolling over onto my hip, I felt frantically for the glass shard I had discovered before Gordy caught me. Found it! My thumb and index finger came together like a vice, trapping the precious fragment between them.

With all my strength I pulled against my wrist binding. Struggled to get enough play to twist one hand. Failed. The glass shard in my fingers clawed fruitlessly at the air. No way to reach the duct tape.

Lying on his belly next to me, Ben raised his head and turned toward me. I slid closer and put my back to him, waving my bound hands at him. My fingers touched his shirt. Pulling at it till I found bare skin, I pressed the glass to his rib cage. Felt him flinch. Willed him to understand.

He grew still. Then with a rustle of jeans, he rolled and shifted until we were back to back. A long moment later, his fingers touched mine.

I squeezed them. Then I walked my fingers up his hand, seeking the tape that bound his wrists. Found it! Heard the grunt of his effort and felt the tape stretch tight as he spread his wrists against it. My thumb located the edge. Maneuvering the glass shard into position, I went to work, imagining that I held a tiny saw. Praying I wouldn't drop it. Urging every ounce of my body's strength into my thumb and index fingers. Something gave. I'd made a tiny cut in the edge of the tape.

Sudden silence grabbed my attention. Gordy had finished emptying his bladder. Footsteps. He was coming back.

Before I could move, familiar musical chimes floated up from below. With a shock, I recognized the tones of my cell phone! The sound of Gordy's footsteps stopped abruptly. My cell phone had been in my purse when Ben knocked it out of my hand. It must still be lying on the promenade below us. And someone was trying to call me! Who? Not a salesman or anyone from work—not at this hour. Underwood? No, I'd never given him my cell number.

Kate. It had to be Kate. She probably got my phone message and wondered why I hadn't called to tell her I was home, like I'd promised.

The ring tones broke off. A moment later, a man's voice barked, "Who?" After a short pause he muttered something I couldn't make out. Then silence. Gordy's footsteps hadn't resumed, so I kept sawing feverishly at Ben's wrist bindings. The cut in the duct tape got a little bigger. From below, the male voice uttered a few more unintelligible words. The duct tape was beginning to yield, and Ben kept spreading his wrists as the length of the cut grew. Gaining more freedom of movement.

As Gordy's footsteps resumed, Ben and I lurched back onto our stomachs. Who had answered my cell phone? The security guard? Or a passerby leaving the bar? What would Kate have told him? Probably nothing very useful. My phone message had been too vague.

Suddenly I felt Gordy's breath on the back of my neck. Had he spotted the piece of glass in my hand? Or noticed the tear in the duct tape around Ben's wrist?

As if in answer, he moved away. Twisting my head, I watched his black shadow creep toward the condo door and stop there. Listening. The silence echoed.

It must be after ten by now. How long would it take Underwood to figure out that Ben wasn't going to show up at the Nagorskis' place? Surely he'd eventually reevaluate my hunch about Harpoon Harry's. I just hoped he wasn't too late

I thought about Gordy's so-called deal. He said he'd let us go if we agreed to his conditions. But realistically, how could he? In spite of what he said, he must know he couldn't count on Ben to take the rap for Jessie's murder. Even if he did "confess" for Rachel's sake, the police would trap him in the lie. Gordy knew that. He'd been arrested enough times to know all about police interrogations. He was just playing mind games with us to keep us in line. As if reading my thoughts, Gordy turned away from the door and glanced our way. He couldn't let any of us go. We knew too much. He'd have to kill us.

When would he do it?

Would he shoot us in the back right here where we lay? That seemed too risky. The security guard would recognize the sound of gunfire and call for help, and the place would be crawling with cops within minutes. Surely Gordy would rather do the deed in some remote place. Hide our bodies. Give himself time to get away before anyone found us.

That meant he'd probably march us out of Fishermen's Village just like he said he would, trying to make us believe he was going to let us go. Most likely he'd do it before Harpoon Harry's closed at midnight so if anyone happened to see us walking out, they'd assume we came from the bar. Besides, Gordy must really be spooked after the security guard—or whoever it was—stopped outside our door. He probably wouldn't wait much longer.

Out of the corner of one eye, I saw his dark shadow move. Then like a ghost, he appeared at Rachel's side. He pulled something from his pocket—a knife, I suddenly realized—and he began to cut her ankle bindings. A few seconds later, he gave her a hushed command. "Stand up, Sweetheart. Don't make a sound." Putting the gun to her back, he marched her toward the condo's exit.

A sudden wide ribbon of light slid across the room, catching us in its glow. Gordy had opened the door. A long moment later, he shoved Rachel out onto the walkway in front of him, leaving the door cracked. In the next instant, I heard a soft ripping sound. Ben sat up, waving his arms in the air like a maniac. Free.

Tearing the tape from his mouth, he whispered, "What did you use to cut through this stuff?"

"Glass. It's all over the floor."

In a flash, he found a piece and sawed my hands free. As I yanked the tape off my face, a board creaked on the walkway. A pause. Another creak. "Let's get behind the door and jump him when he comes in," Ben whispered.

"No," I hissed. "He'll see we're gone as soon as he opens the door—and he's got Rachel! Get back down. Press the tape back on your face like it was. Make your hands look like they're still bound."

Another board creaked, much closer. "After Rachel's back, that's when we've got to overpower him," I whispered. "He can't let us go, Ben, no matter what he said."

"I know."

"I think he'll try to march us out of Fishermen's Village pretty soon. And to do that, he'll need to loosen the bindings on our ankles. With luck, he'll set the pistol down for a moment, and that'll be our chance. Let's have a signal. Three high little whimpers. One, two, three, CHARGE."

"Got it," Ben whispered.

Curling up onto my side, I slashed at my ankle bindings. Just as the last inch of duct tape gave way, the door creaked. A moment later, we were bathed in light.

Chapter Thirty-eight

Shoving Rachel into the room ahead of him, Gordy pulled the door closed behind him. For a nerve-wracking minute he stood still. I held my breath. Had he seen us flip back into position? No! His first command was to Rachel.

"Get over there!" he ordered. With his gun in her ribs, he prodded the girl into the corner by the sliding door. "Sit down," he ordered. "Get your back against the wall." Like a zombie, she obeyed.

"OK, gang, it's time," he announced softy. He shifted his pistol to his left hand and pulled a small knife from his pocket. "I'm going to cut the bindings on your feet. You don't try anything smart, you all walk out of here alive. Got that?"

I nodded as if I meant it, wondering all the while how much time I had before he discovered I was free. As he started toward me, I prayed he would set his gun down before he reached for my ankle bindings. Instead, *oh no!* He was going to check my wrists! It was now or never! I let out three high-pitched whimpers. One-two-three-GO!

In a single motion, I rolled away from him, pulled my knees to my chest, and kicked at him with all my strength, trying to knock the gun out of his hand. I heard him grunt as I made contact, but he hung onto the weapon. I glimpsed its dark shadow as it came toward the side of my head.

It never struck. The next thing I knew, Ben and his father were flailing at each other in the middle of floor. Clambering to my feet, I stood over them, waiting for a chance to spring at Gordy without getting Ben. Where was Gordy's knife? Not in his hand! I scoured the floor with my fingers. Couldn't find it.

Gordy swung his pistol at his son's head. Ben ducked in time. In the same instant, I saw my chance and dove for Gordy's arm. The gun flew out of his hand. I scrambled for it, but he grabbed my ankle, and I tumbled to the floor. Shards of glass sliced my arms as I landed. In the corner, Rachel had stood up, but still huddled against the wall, whimpering through the duct tape over her mouth.

Ben tackled his father around the waist, but Gordy kept crawling toward the gun, dragging his son along. I rolled toward the weapon. Gordy saw me, and I braced for the impact, but it didn't happen. Somehow Ben had managed to hang on, and now his hands had found his father's throat.

It took a mere instant for Gordy to break his son's hold, but it was long enough for me to snatch up the pistol and scramble to my feet. All rationality had left me. Terror and rage wiped out every sane thought. I pointed the weapon at Gordy's chest, using both my trembling hands, but I hesitated a moment too long. Gordy picked Ben up and hurled him like a sack of flour at my legs. We crashed to the floor together, and the gun slid from my grasp.

A shadow flew in front of my eyes, and I heard a moan like the cry of a wounded animal. Whirling around, I saw Gordy doubled over on the floor grasping his groin. Rachel stood over him, kicking at his hands without mercy, grunts of rage escaping through her taped lips. *You go, Girl!*

Frantically, I searched the area where the weapon had landed. It wasn't there.

From behind me, Ben commanded, "Stand back, Anna." Whirling around, I discovered what had happened to the gun. Ben now gripped it firmly in both hands, and he pointed it straight at his father's chest. "Back off, Rachel," he ordered. "He's mine."

Groaning, Gordy staggered to a standing position, his back to the soft glow around the plywood that covered the glass slider. "Easy, Son," he said, transforming himself before our eyes into the genial fellow I once thought I knew. "You wouldn't shoot your own father now, would you?"

Ben's chest heaved, but the gun stayed steady in his hand. "Yes, Father, I would. Raise your arms high and don't move."

Rachel had stepped away from Gordy. Now she backed up to me where I stood near the side wall. Something very sharp touched my wrist. Startled, I looked down. Rachel's hands were still taped securely behind her back, but her fingers clutched Gordy's small knife! I grabbed it, cut her hands free, and dropped the knife into my pocket.

Stealing a quick glance at us, Ben said firmly, "Rachel, get out of here. You too, Anna. I don't want you to see this. Go down to Harpoon Harry's. Tell someone to call for help."

"Do as he says, Rachel," I said. "Go! I need to stay here."

Wild-eyed, the girl snatched the tape from her mouth. "Come with me," she pleaded.

"No, you go on." I pointed beyond Ben to the condo door. "As soon as you get to the bottom of the stairs, start screaming for help."

After an anguished moment, she turned and hurried toward the door, touching the wall with one hand to steady herself. As she drew parallel to Ben, she paused to look at him, then passed behind his back toward the door. Ben never took his gaze from his father.

Rachel cracked open the door, letting in a narrow swath of illumination. I watched her slip out. And stifled a gasp as a large hand grabbed the edge of the door high above her head. A uniformed policeman slid in, followed soundlessly by half a dozen others. Underwood must have called in reinforcements. Finally! Weapons drawn, they took in the scene at a glance and aimed at Ben's back. The officer who had been the first to enter commanded, "Drop the gun, Ben."

Ben's whole body twitched with surprise and he glanced back over his shoulder. Instantly, his head snapped back toward his father, and I saw his finger tense on the trigger. In that split second, words Ben had said earlier raced through my mind. "There's no way out of this for me." "I guess I can tell you about it; it doesn't matter anyway." "Peace is a phantom; only death is real." He had given up. What he told me didn't matter because he didn't intend to be around for long. Suicide had been his plan all along!

But first he was going to kill his father!

"No!" I screamed, as much to the police as to Ben. Propelled by sheer instinct, I leaped between him and Gordy. "You don't have to kill your father," I shrieked. "The police are here to arrest him."

"Get out of the way, Anna," Ben said, edging sideways.

Ignoring the armed and helmeted team who fanned into the room, I focused only on Ben. My whole body shook, but I did my best to make my voice strong enough to carry throughout the room. "They're here to arrest your father for the murder of your brother. You need to tell these officers what you told me—that you saw your father kill Jessie. And that you ran away because he realized you had witnessed the whole thing."

Ben still pointed the pistol at me, but I kept talking. "You also need to tell them that when you were eight years old, you saw your father murder your youngest brother, Leon. And Jessie found out about it. That's why your father killed him."

I sensed some kind of action behind me, but I didn't take my eyes off Ben. "Rachel will tell the police that Gordon Tolliver kidnapped her and kept her as a hostage. And I'll testify that he tied us all up—you and me and Rachel—and held us at gunpoint here in this condo. When you give the police the pistol you're holding, they'll find your father's fingerprints all over it."

Something was definitely going on behind me, and Ben was watching it, but I just kept talking. "None of this is your fault, Ben. Don't throw your life away"

"My life ain't worth shit."

"That's not true. Your life is worth a whole lot to me. And to Rachel. And . . . to Coach Jack."

One of the policemen now spoke to Ben very gently. "We have your father in handcuffs now, Son. He can't hurt you anymore. You won't need that gun."

Turning to follow Ben's gaze, I saw what he had been watching. Gordy was indeed in handcuffs and firmly in the grasp of two burly policemen.

Ben stared at his father for a long time. Then without a word, he pointed the gun at the floor and handed it, butt first, to me.

Chapter Thirty-nine

The questioning at the police station lasted well into the night. To my surprise, Underwood apologized for discounting my theory that "Harry's" meant Harpoon Harry's. "Ten o'clock passed and Ben didn't turn up," the detective explained. "Then I got a call from the security guard at Fish Village. He said he found your purse when some minister called your cell phone with a wild tale about a runaway teen and a killer. I sent the SWAT team."

"Thank God!"

I told the detective everything that had happened since I last saw him, beginning with my visit to Tiffany's former neighbor and her shocking revelation about Ben and Jessie's epileptic younger brother. I explained how my study of Ben's poems led to my discovery that his most obscure symbols referred to his father. Underwood was especially interested in my theory that someone at Sunset Days Care Center provided Gordy with an alibi because they were partners in stealing prescription drugs.

"That ties in with our suspicions about the BMW driver you put us onto," he said. "We're about to make him for his connection to a gang that's selling Oxycontin and other prescription drugs from a convenience store in Fort Myers."

By the time a patrolman finally escorted me home, Gordy had been carted off to jail and Ben had reluctantly agreed to allow a soft-spoken therapist from Charlotte Behavioral Healthcare to take him to their Crisis Stabilization Unit. When I questioned Underwood about Jack Braxton, he asked, "Do you want to press charges against him for holding you hostage at his house that night?"

"No," I said quickly.

"OK. Get some rest," he said.

I did. I fell into bed exhausted and didn't move until the phone rang.

"I bet I woke you, and I'm sorry." I recognized the voice of the Guardian Ad Litem Coordinator. "I need to tell you that a Shelter Hearing for the Tolliver case is on the court docket for 10:30 this morning."

A shelter hearing. This morning! Of course. Florida law requires this type of hearing within twenty-four hours any time children are taken from their home or moved to a new placement. "That's just over two hours from now," I said, doing my best to regain consciousness.

"That's why I called."

"OK, I'll be there." I was waking up fast. I only had two hours to find out what DCF planned to do with Ben—and to try to influence their decision. I began by calling the protective investigator assigned to the case, Paul Frost. He'd been in touch with Ben's therapist at the Crisis Stabilization Unit, who said Ben had agreed to regular outpatient counseling and could be released to a home where he would receive adequate emotional support.

"He needs to go back to Candy and George Owen," I said.

"Sure, that would be ideal," Paul said. "But Melody Kahn, his case manager, says the Owens' house is already maxed out. Ben qualifies for a therapeutic placement, where the foster family has had training in parenting children with emotional problems. Melody still hopes to make that happen, but there aren't any homes like that available in Charlotte County, so Ben may end up in Fort Myers or even Sarasota."

I panicked. "He'll be getting therapy from Charlotte Behavioral Center. What he needs more than anything is stability and love. He's already lived in seven foster homes, Paul, not to mention his most recent placement with a father who's a murderer. Melody can't be thinking about putting him in yet another foster home, therapeutic or not!"

"Like I said, it's not the first choice, but I don't know if anything can be done about it."

"Well I'm sure going to try!"

I spent the next hour and a half on the phone. By the time I arrived at the courthouse, I had worked out a more acceptable solution. George Owen would squeeze his computer station into their master bedroom and convert his small office/den into a bedroom for Ben. Kate and some members of our congregation would scrounge a twin bed and dresser somewhere and round up volunteers to move furniture. Melody still voiced concern that the Owens' house would be overcrowded, but she finally agreed it was the best option, at least for the time being. All that remained was to get the judge's OK.

When I arrived in Judge Walton's courtroom, the half dozen pew-like benches in the small visitors' section were nearly full, but I squeezed into one of the few empty spaces. At 10:25 our Guardian Ad Litem lawyer ambled through one of the gates in the "bar," the low wall that separates the official legal proceedings from the onlookers. She seated herself at one of the two tables that faced the judge. Like the other lawyers involved in the case, she had the right to raise objections and to call and question witnesses. I had come to look upon her as my lifeline whenever I was asked to testify. Melody Kahn and Paul Frost meandered into position at the DCF table along the right wall. DCF lawyer Ted Garman, whose will was rarely challenged in this setting, stood locked in conversation with a gentleman I didn't recognize. After a quick glance at his watch, the man hurried out of the court, made his way through the visitors' gallery, and disappeared beyond the double doors that led to the main corridor. Garman glanced toward me, and I felt a vague sense of unease.

At ten-thirty sharp, the bailiff ordered, "All present, please rise." Judge Walton, whose solemn black robe seemed at odds with his kind face and farmer-boy gait, took his place on the high bench, set down his coffee cup, gave a light rap with his gavel, and declared court in session.

The whole procedure, which had been foreign to me when I first began volunteering with the Guardian Ad Litem program, was now familiar. The DCF lawyer basically ran the show. Garman spoke so fast I'd had trouble understanding him at first, but now I knew what to listen for. "Number 04-976-D-CJ, Tolliver," he intoned. That was the signal for all of us who were party to the case to pass through the low gate and take our positions in the court.

Quickly, I took my seat next to our Guardian Ad Litem lawyer, facing the judge. Melody Kahn and Paul Frost, the DCF staff assigned to the case, were already in place next to Garman at their table along the wall to my right. The table to my left, which also faced the judge, was reserved for parents of the children and their lawyers. Today the only person who came to this table was Gordy's court-appointed lawyer. After stating his name, he added, "Attorney for the Father, who can't be present because he is appearing in another courtroom at this time."

"Arraignment," our lawyer whispered to me. "They're charging him with First Degree."

My stomach cramped with nerves, and I sternly ordered myself to relax. The court procedure should be quick and easy. As usual, the hard work had been done behind the scenes. Garman would rattle off a battery of routine questions to the protective investigator and case manager and then ask their recommendation regarding Ben's placement. They would give the answer we had all agreed upon. I'd be sworn in, and Garman would ask me if I concurred with their recommendation. I'd say yes. In addition, I'd request counseling for Ben. The Judge would it order it all done, and he'd set the date for the next hearing. The whole thing shouldn't take over five minutes.

Only it didn't go that way. Instead of following his usual procedure, the DCF lawyer addressed the judge. "Your Honor, something unexpected has come up that may affect the decisions to be made today. May I approach the bench?"

Now what? For what seemed like an hour, but was probably only three or four minutes, the judge held an inaudible conference with Garman. Then the DCF lawyer turned to face the gallery. "Is John Braxton present in the courtroom?" he asked.

Stunned, I whirled around to survey the rest of the visitors' gallery and blinked in amazement at the familiar figure who had been standing at the back wall. He moved forward, followed by the man I had seen talking with Garman earlier.

"Come to the witness stand, Sir," Garman instructed.

With all eyes on them, the two men made their way through the low gate. Jack climbed up into the witness box. The judge swore him in, then turned to the other man, who had stepped to the center podium, facing the judge.

"Lester Abrams, attorney for John Braxton," he said.

"You may proceed," Judge Walton said with a nod.

After having Jack state his name, Abrams said, "What is your relationship to the child, Benjamin Tolliver?"

"I have reason to believe I am Ben's biological father."

Chapter Forty

Silencing the audible stir that erupted in the gallery after Jack's incredible revelation, Judge Walton rapped his gavel. Jack continued. "As I said, I believe I am Ben's biological father, and if this proves to be true, I wish to request custody of my son."

"What is the basis for your paternity claim?" his lawyer asked.

Jack took a deep breath. "Sixteen years ago, when I was a junior in high school, I had one date with a senior girl named Tiffany Oakes. In hindsight, I think she just went out with me to taunt her boyfriend, Gordon Tolliver, but we had sex. Two months later, she announced that she was pregnant and that she and Tolliver were getting married. I asked her if the child could be mine, but she just laughed and told me she had worn protection. At the time, of course, I was relieved." He paused. Swallowed hard. "Later I married and had a son."

A son! How could Jack have a son? On our first date, I'd asked if he had children, and he'd said no!

"Twenty-eight months ago," Jack continued, "my wife and son were killed in an auto accident in Atlanta. For awhile, I pretty much fell to pieces. But after I finally got hold of myself, I began wondering about Tiffany's baby—whether her child could possibly be mine. I mean, she could have been lying about wearing protection. I uh . . . really didn't know what I'd do if the child was mine. I just wanted to know. So I tracked down Tiffany's address through friends of the family who still lived in our old neighborhood . When I saw Ben, I knew he was my son. He has my coloring, the same eyes, and I . . . ."

Abrams stopped him. "Do you have any proof he's your son—other than thinking he looks like you?"

"I ordered a paternity test on line. TTL Labs. Ben um . . . stayed with me for a few days after he ran away from home, and I took the required swab from inside his cheek one night while he slept. TTL wouldn't give me the results over the phone, but with your help"—he looked to his lawyer—"I understand we can get them by fax within a couple hours."

"Mr. Braxton," Abrams continued, "you have indicated that you request custody of Benjamin if an accredited paternity test shows that he is your son. Is that correct?"

"Yes, Sir."

"Are you in a position to provide a stable home for him?"

"Yes, Sir. I own a home. I have a reliable income. And I would"—Jack stopped to clear his throat—"I would do my best to be a good father to him."

"Pass the witness," Abrams said.

When the judge turned to the DCF lawyer, the usually unflappable Garman seemed too surprised to get his thoughts together. "No questions, Your Honor."

Looking to our table, the judge asked, "What about the Guardian Ad Litem?" Our lawyer turned to me. I wanted to ask a hundred things, but not here in this courtroom. I shook my head.

Judge Walton studied the paperwork in front of him, stroked his chin for what seemed forever, and finally turned to the DCF lawyer. "Do you have a proposal, Mr. Garman?"

"Your Honor, if we could continue this hearing until this afternoon's session, we might have a conclusive answer as to the paternity in question."

The judge gave a quick nod. "We will continue this hearing at two o'clock this afternoon." He turned to Garman. "Next case."

I rushed through the visitors' gallery into the short hallway that buffered the courtroom from the main corridor. I wasn't going to let Jack escape without talking to me.

A moment later, he burst through the door. When he saw me, he stopped. For a very long moment, we gazed at each other, struck dumb, it seemed, by all that had happened and by the earth-shaking revelations of the morning. Finally I blurted, "Oh, Jack! You didn't tell me about your son!"

His face twisted in anguish, "I should have. I just couldn't get the words out of my mouth."

I didn't know what to say. So many things made sense now. Why Jack volunteered to coach Pop Warner. Why he had taken such a special interest in Ben—even breaking the law to give him sanctuary after he ran away. All these thoughts competed for attention in my brain, but what came out of my mouth was simply, "What was your son's name?"

"Richard. We called him Rick." He looked away. "About what happened at my house that night . . . well, thanks for not pressing charges."

I couldn't look at him either. "You did what you had to do, I guess."

"I'm truly sorry. When you raised the possibility that Rachel could be using her friend's computer, it dawned on me that Ben might have received an email from her. I had to find out. It didn't take me long to track Ben's activity on my computer, and sure enough, there was Rachel's email warning him that you'd been asking questions about me. You'd already told me Mrs. Owen had alerted the police to check the friend's computer. I knew it wouldn't take them long to find the email, and they'd show up on my doorstep any minute. When the doorbell rang, I panicked."

I dragged my gaze back up to his face and found his eyes looking into mine. "I wasn't thinking straight," he said. "I knew the police had come to arrest me. I'd be accused of abducting Ben—and maybe even of killing his brother. And I was desperate to find him—not just to clear my name, but to talk him into turning himself in before he made his chances ten times worse."

"You thought he killed Jessie?"

"He refused to talk about it, so yeah, that's what I figured. But when I pressed him to go to the police voluntarily, he clammed up."

"He'd had too many bad experiences with the law."

"I know that now." Taking my elbow, he pulled me out of the center of the hallway, where a string of people still flowed out of the courtroom. Then awkwardly, he dropped his arm, leaving a tingling spot where his hand had been.

"And you?" I asked quickly. "Will you be charged with anything?"

"No. My neighbor—the one whose car I, um, borrowed—says he won't press charges." One corner of his lips turned up slightly. "I really did take good care of his house after the hurricane hit, and I returned his car unharmed."

"So you're free?"

"Seems that way. And luckier than I deserve. Underwood said he could arrest me on any one of several charges, but he decided not to. He's a decent fellow, really."

"He can be." But something still bothered me. "May I ask you a question?"

"Shoot."

"What were you doing at Tiffany Tolliver's trailer the morning she died?" Watching his eyebrows shoot up in surprise, I added, "A neighbor saw you."

He gave me that half smile that had drawn me to him so many eons ago. "You don't miss much, do you?" When I didn't respond, he said, "I went to see if she had any idea where Ben could be. Then I asked her if she'd told me the truth about, um, using protection. She admitted she'd lied about that because she wanted Gordy to marry her. He was pretty hot stuff in high school, at least in certain crowds. I told her I thought Ben was my son, and if I could prove it, I was going to petition for the right to spend time with him." He wiped his hand across his brow. "I left her in tears."

I thought back to that morning. I'd stopped by the trailer on my way to work to show Tiffany and Gordy Ben's poems. Tiffany must have recognized the reference to Forsaken Angel and Bulldog. Connected the dots. Realized her husband had killed Leon—and maybe Jessie too. That's probably when she started popping Xanax. Thus fortified, she called me. Asked me to meet her so she could tell me something about the poems. Then Jack showed up threatening to take Ben from her—or at least to sue for shared custody. And the Oxycontin was handy. No wonder she wanted to stop the pain.

"I'm sorry about Tiffany," Jack said. "Looking back, I think she was pretty loopy that morning, but I didn't realize it at the time."

He glanced sideways, and I was belatedly aware of his lawyer who hovered a few feet away. Introducing Abrams, Jack said, "We're on the way to his law office. Ben's case manager, Melody Kahn, said she'd come as soon as she finishes testifying in her other cases. By the time she arrives, I hope to have the results of the paternity test. Then we'll figure out where to go from there. About Ben I mean. I'd like you to come too."

"Oh! Ummm . . . ."

"To represent Ben's interests," he added quickly.

"I guess I could." In truth, wild horses couldn't have kept me away.

Chapter Forty-one

In the portable building that had been serving as the makeshift office of Attorney Les Abrams since the hurricane, all heads turned toward the gentle whir of the fax machine. The lawyer watched it clunk into silence, then pulled out a legal sized sheet of paper and read it quickly, his face a well-trained expressionless mask. He reached across his desk and handed it to Jack, who was seated in one of the two available client chairs. I occupied the other one, my eyes glued to Jack's face as he read.

Jack stared at the sheet a long moment. Then he dropped his head into his hands, propping his elbows on his knees. The paper slid to the floor. Stooping to pick it up, Abrams shook his balding head at me.

For a long time, no one spoke. A sharp knock broke the painful silence and Melody Kahn burst in, looking as usual as if she just escaped from a tornado. As the case manager's gaze shifted from Jack to me and back to Jack, Abrams handed her the fax. She read it quickly, then studied Jack for a few moments without speaking. He did not look up. Melody crossed the tiny office and planted her feet in front of him. "So you're not the father," she said with typical bluntness.

Jack glanced at her, then lowered his head again. Like someone waking from a dream, he murmured, "I was so sure he was my son. I can't believe he's Gordy's kid. He looks so much more like me."

Because he's fair-skinned and blue eyed. But so was Tiffany. In truth, Ben looked more like his mother than either of the men who claimed paternity.

Kahn frowned at him. "You really wanted that emotionally-disturbed hunk of trouble for a son?" I started to tell the insensitive shrew to shut her face, but Jack cut me off.

"Yeah, I did." His hands clenched his knees.

"You still want him?"

Jack looked up at her. "What do you mean?"

"Parenting isn't all about biology, you know," she said, and some of the harshness left her face. "There's foster parenting, even adoption--if you're serious about taking him on." When he didn't respond, she added, "Or do you only want him if he's carrying your genes?"

Jack frowned. "He already has a good home with the Owens. What right do I have to pull him away from that?"

Melody ran her fingers through her hair, accenting the impression that she'd just stepped out of a windstorm. "Yes, he'll have a good home—for now. But Candy and George will never adopt him. Their life mission—God bless them—is foster care. They're busy impacting the lives of dozens of kids—and we need them desperately. But they aren't *forever* parents. They can't be. When Ben turns eighteen three years from now, he'll age out of the system. Sure, the state will help him pay for college if he chooses to go—and it appears he's got the brains to do that. But he won't have a home to come back to on vacations. The Owens' house will be filled with other kids who need them. George and Candy won't be at his wedding—not as parents anyway. They can't be grandparents to his children."

Silence echoed through the room. Finally Jack spoke in a voice so low I had to strain to hear. "Could I actually do that—adopt him?"

"If you mean, do you have what it takes to parent a kid who's got a host of problems, I can't answer that. But if you mean, will the system let you, the most likely answer is yes. His mother is dead. His father is charged with first-degree murder, and Detective Underwood says they have more than enough evidence to convict him. In a situation like this, termination of parental rights will be virtually automatic. The process will take some time, of course, but he'll almost certainly become eligible for adoption. If he had any relatives who could—or would—take him in, we'd have found them long ago."

"You said the process takes time," Jack said. "How long?"

"Six months to a year for adoption if all goes smoothly. But in the meantime, he's eligible for foster care right now." She ran her hand through her hair again. "Well, not quite right now. We'd have to do a home study—a background check—that sort of thing. But we can usually do that pretty fast when we need to."

"A background check." Jack's voice had turned hollow and his body slumped.

"You got a problem with a background check?" Melody asked sharply.

Jack studied his hands. "It'll show that I have two DUI's and a Drunk and Disorderly on my record. And that I spent three months in rehab. Like I told the judge, I had a really bad time after my wife and son were killed. I started drinking. A lot. Lost my job. Finally, I realized I had to get my life together, and I checked myself into rehab. After I got out, I began to think about Tiffany and the baby she had fifteen years ago."

"You go to AA?" Kahn quizzed.

"At least three times a week, even while I've been hiding out."

"How long since your last alcoholic drink?"

"Ten months and two weeks."

The case manager paced the short length of the office, absently rolling up the fax as if it were a diploma. She stopped in front of Jack. "Mr. Braxton," she said with a half smile, "it's not our department's policy to reject a qualified foster parent because he doesn't drink. We'd have to check it out, make sure your sobriety is for real. We'd talk to people who know you, and we'd probably ask you to subject yourself to random urine tests for awhile."

Jack had straightened up. "No problem."

"Think about it," Melody told him. "Take your time. It's a big decision." She handed him the rolled-up fax.

Jack didn't bother to unroll it. "I need to talk with Ben."

"Not today, you don't," Melody said quickly. "Even if you decide to apply for foster care, we can't make that happen till the home study is done. In the meantime, we'll place Ben with the Owens. That's the only thing we'll try to accomplish in this afternoon's hearing. In a few weeks, there will be another hearing to set some longer-term goals for Ben's care. By then, we should have completed your home study."

"I need to talk to him today," Jack insisted, and his voice was a lot stronger. "The press is going to be all over this story. I don't want Ben to find out in the newspaper that I claimed to be his father. He needs to hear that from me."

Melody studied him with pursed lips, then sighed. "I'll see if I can arrange it with the Crisis Stabilization Unit."

By one forty-five, the crowd in the courtroom's gallery had thinned out, and Kate joined me in the front seat of the center section. I'd called her earlier to thank her for the phone call that saved my life. "I'm glad you could come," I told her.

"I wouldn't miss it for the world," she said. "Thanks for inviting me."

I smiled at her. "After this is all over, how about coming to my house for dinner sometime? I'll actually cook. No meatloaf, chicken casseroles, or Jell-O salad."

"You're on."

At five minutes till two, Ted Garman ambled to the DCF table. I craned my neck to scan the visitor's gallery and spotted Jack in the back row, ramrod straight, but fidgety and pale. Our eyes met, and he held up crossed fingers. I returned the gesture. On the stroke of two, Judge Walton entered, and Garman called the Tolliver case.

I took my place next to our lawyer at the Guardian table. Protective Investigator Paul Frost stepped over to the DCF table, but there was no sign of his case manager.. Then to my surprise, Melody Kahn burst through the double doors and strode up the aisle with Ben in trail, followed by Candy and George Owen! Ben stole a furtive glance at Jack as he passed, then looked quickly away. The trio slid in next to Kate in the front row of the visitors' section as Melody hurried on to the DCF table.

The case progressed with breathtaking speed as Garman peppered Melody with the regular battery of questions—questions that seemed almost rote to anyone who spent much time in the Dependency Court. "What is your recommendation for the placement of this child?" he asked her.

In a virtual monotone, Melody stated that because of the death of his mother and the incarceration of his father, she recommended that Ben be placed in foster care. After several more questions received the expected answers, he intoned, "Is there a child in the case over the age of thirteen who wishes to make a statement?"

"Yes," Melody answered. Garman snapped his head toward her in obvious surprise. The question was routine, and the answer was usually no. "Ben Tolliver has requested permission to make a statement," Melody explained.

A hush fell over the gallery as the case manager crossed the courtroom to open the gate for Ben. She gave him an encouraging smile, but he kept his gaze straight ahead as she escorted him to the steps leading to the high stand next to the judge. He stood awkwardly in the witness box until Judge Walton said gently, "You may sit down. And raise your right hand, please."

After the judge swore Ben in, Garman moved to the center microphone. "State your name please." His voice was firm, but not unkind.

"Ben Tolliver." Although he spoke clearly, his hands twisted nervously.

"How old are you?"

"Fifteen."

"Ben, we are recommending that you return to the same foster home where you stayed before you moved in with your parents three months ago," he said. "Do you understand what I'm saying?"

"Yes, Sir." Ben shuffled in his seat. His Adams apple jumped as he swallowed.

"Is there something you wish to tell the court about that?"

"No, Sir. Not about that."

Garman glanced at Kahn. In profile, I could see his raised eyebrows. Turning back to Ben, he said, "But you do wish to make a statement to the court?"

"Yes, Sir. I . . . um . . . no offense to the Owens." He looked out at Candy and George. "You are cool foster parents." I saw Garman flinch—names of foster parents were never supposed to be mentioned in court proceedings. Ben turned and spoke directly to the judge. "I just want to say that as soon as I can, I would like to live with a real father." He faltered a moment, then added, "I don't mean my biological father."

Judge Walton frowned. "Could you explain what you do mean?"

Ben straightened, placing his hands palm down on the witness stand. "I mean my biological father was never a real father to me. I'd like to live with someone who would be. I'd be grateful to stay with the Owens for now, but as soon as I can, I'd like to live with Coach Jack Braxton and eventually to be adopted by him . . . if he still wants me."

Garman turned to Kahn and spread his hands in a gesture that said, *What do I do now?*

"We're working on that," she told him.

Garman faced the judge. "We're working on that, Your Honor," he said. "In the meantime, we need an order to return him to foster care."

I motioned frantically to our lawyer. Noticing, the judge turned directly to me. "Does the Guardian Ad Litem wish to add something?"

"Yes, your Honor," I said. "We also need an order for psychological counseling."

"So ordered," said the judge. "Next case."

As Ben returned to the gallery, Jack rose to meet him. The two of them faced each other, both looking as if they wanted to reach out, neither mustering the nerve. Jack raised his palm. "Give me five, Ben," he said with a shaky grin.

Ben slapped his hand. "See you, Coach."

"Soon," Jack said.

My gaze followed Ben as he left the courtroom, flanked by Candy and George Owen. Jack was so busy watching Ben, he didn't seem to notice when I stepped up beside him. "So much for taking your time with the decision," I murmured to him.

He turned to me, his cheeks wet. "I don't need time."

We stood there a moment, neither of us seeming able to find words. I started for the door.

"Anna, wait," Jack said. "About our dinner date that ended in such a disaster, would you . . . I mean, do you think we could . . . well . . . start over?"

"I would like that," I said. "I would like that very much," I added as we walked out of the courtroom together.

AUTHOR'S NOTE

Runaway Poet is pure fiction.

And yet much of this story is true. The foster care system. The Dependency Court. Undiagnosed fetal alcohol syndrome and its devastating effects. Drug abuse and the challenge of recovery. Hurricane Charley and life in a FEMA trailer. The unsung heroes—volunteers—who advocate for abused, neglected, and abandoned children. All true. Much of the geography is also true, although I have created some fictional streets. Peace River United Church and Charlotte Family Practice are fictitious.

The characters and the events that make up the plot are all fiction.

ACKNOWLEDGMENTS

My special thanks goes to each of the following people:

Detective Harvey Ayers, Punta Gorda, Florida, Police Department for walking me through police procedures

Reverend Bill Klossner, volunteer Police Chaplain and Pastor of Congregational United Church, Punta Gorda, Florida, for additional insight into police protocols and a short course on Pop Warner football

Emily Pritchard, Child Advocacy Coordinator, Guardian Ad Litem Program, Charlotte County, Florida, for her careful reading of the manuscript and her enthusiastic support

faithful critics Peg Nagel, Barb Cooper, Beth Roper, and Reverend Trish Greeves

my husband Don for technical, literary, emotional and other support in ways far too numerous to name.

ABOUT THE AUTHOR

Like the story's central character, Myra Nagel has worked as a volunteer Guardian Ad Litem in Charlotte County, Florida, where she and her husband Don reside. In 2004, she lived through the ravages of Hurricane Charley. A United Church of Christ minister, she has served churches in Virginia and Florida. She is the author of the mystery novel, **Downside Seven** and several non-fiction books including **Journey to the Cross, Deliver Us From Evil** and *What to Do Instead of Screaming.*

Myra is donating her proceeds from the sale of *Runaway Poet* to **Voices for Kids of Southwest Florida**, an organization dedicated to improving the lives of the abused, neglected, and abandoned children who come under the protection of Southwest Florida's courts.

www.myranagel.com

Made in the USA
Charleston, SC
30 May 2013